TO LOVE A HIGHLAND LAIRD

Heart of a Scot, Book One
Third Edition

COLLETTE CAMERON

Blue Rose Romance®
Portland, Oregon

Sweet-to-Spicy Timeless Romance®

TO LOVE A HIGHLAND LAIRD
Heart of a Scot
Copyright © 2021 Collette Cameron®
Cover Art: Sheri McGathy

Attn: Permissions Coordinator
Blue Rose Romance®
8420 N Ivanhoe # 83054
Portland, Oregon 97203

eBook ISBN: 9781954307681
Paperback ISBN: 9781954307698

collettecameron.com

"Ah, my love, my precious love. All will be well,
I vow. Somehow I shall make it so."

Other Collette Cameron Books

Heart of a Scot
To Love a Highland Laird
To Redeem a Highland Rogue
To Seduce a Highland Scoundrel
To Woo a Highland Warrior
To Enchant a Highland Earl
To Defy a Highland Duke
To Marry a Highland Marauder
To Bargain with a Highland Buccaneer
A Christmas Kiss for the Highlander

Check out Collette's Other Series
Daughters of Desire (Scandalous Ladies)
Highland Heather Romancing a Scot
The Blue Rose Regency Romances:
The Culpepper Misses
Castle Brides
Seductive Scoundrels
The Honorable Rogues®

Collections
Lords in Love
The Honorable Rogues® Books 1-3
The Honorable Rogues® Books 4-6
Seductive Scoundrels Series Books 1-3
Seductive Scoundrels Series Books 4-6
The Blue Rose Regency Romances-
The Culpepper Misses Series 1-2

Dedication

To my darling Grandpa Cameron from
whom I borrowed my *nom de plume.*
I share your love of songbirds, tea, and
adoration of all things Scottish.
Till we meet again—

Prologue

Dunrangour Tower, Scottish Highlands
6 September, 1701

"Logan, my boy, ye sign here." Artair Rutherford pointed to an empty space below his and Laird Roderick Findlay's bold, slanted signature.

Och, cow turds.

Despite his frustration, Logan obediently propped his battered toy sword against the table's leg. After carefully dipping the quill into the inkwell, he lifted his uncertain gaze to his father.

"My full name, Da?"

"Aye, Son."

"And when I do, it means I must wed her? When

I'm a mon?" He pointed the quill at a wee lassie in an elaborate wooden cradle, gnawing on her wet fist.

"Aye, lad." Inclining his head, Da patted Logan's shoulder, the gesture more prodding than reassuring. "She'll be yer wife."

Logan sucked in his cheeks and crimped his mouth, mutinously. "I dinna want to marry her."

What need have I for a wife? Da disna have one.

"Ye're no' actually marryin' her right now, Son," Da cajoled gently. "Ye're just agreein' to later, when ye're both adults."

That brought Logan a little relief. "I still dinna want to."

"It's a good match. A brilliant one, truth to tell." Bending over a little, Da put a hand on Logan's shoulder and peered intently into his eyes. "But more importantly, Son, the union benefits Scotland. Ye should be proud."

Findlay, Dunrangour's giant of a laird, snorted loud as a draft horse and shook his shaggy blond mane. "So say some."

Craning his neck, Logan gulped and took a

reflexive step backward.

"Ever heard such a colossal *jobby* before, Fergus and Hamish?" Findlay bit out, his jaw muscles jumping and huge hands clenched into powerful balls.

Such a pile of shite?

Which part?

The stupid match or the benefitin' Scotland part?

A pair of Dunrangour clansmen acting as witnesses, their flinty gazes unyielding and faces granite hard, grunted and smirked their agreement.

"Nae, canna say I have, Findlay," the one called Hamish said, giving Da an evil scowl.

"And of course, Mayra's dowry—particularly the land portion—be of nae interest to ye, be it, Rutherford? But, ye canna touch either yet, can ye? No' until our children actually wed. And then it'll be the lad's to do with as he pleases, no' yers. How that must set yer teeth on edge and stick in yer greedy craw."

Findlay's low chuckle, more sinister than humorous, filled the tense silence. Satisfaction, or mayhap even gloating, tinged his words and ignited his vivid blue eyes.

Viking eyes.

Ruthless and cold and unforgiving.

Da said Dunrangour's laird was descended from the barbaric Norsemen, and Logan could well believe it.

His sweet-faced wife didn't join in his mirth. If anything, she hunched deeper into her chair, more distraught.

"Asinine requirin' me to provide half of the lass' marriage settlement now. Reeks of extortion." Findlay's hefty glower encompassed Da and Mr. Hyde, the king's agent.

Logan scrunched his forehead and mouth, gazing between the wrathful laird and his gentle lady.

Didn't they want this stupid troth thing either?

As a lad, he couldn't disobey Da's order, but they were grown-ups. And adults could do what they wanted.

Why didn't they just say no then?

He'd be well-pleased if they did.

He looked at the slobbering baby again and couldn't prevent his lip curling.

Reddish brows drawn into such a severe vee they almost touched, Da glared hard at Findlay until Logan's tugging on his coat finally drew his father's attention.

"What's a cowry, Da?"

"Dowry." His father's stern features softened a wee bit. "It's a legal token promisin' ye and the lass will wed."

A sneer curled Findlay's mouth as he crossed his thick arms and planted a bulging shoulder against the fireplace. "I'd call it extortion and a forced match between a wee six-year-old lad and an infant lass. Neither of which have any say in their futures."

"Give careful thought to yer words, Findlay. Some might consider them and yer attitude treasonous. Ye wouldna want a hint of anythin' untoward to reach His Majesty's ears, would ye now?" Mr. Hyde *tsked* disapprovingly, his eyes gone squinty and suspicious. His pointy nostrils even twitched in reproach.

Like a giant wharf rat.

Logan pinched his nose and pointed his face away. Reeking of dirty feet, stale sweat, and rotting teeth, the agent stank worse than Leith's docks.

Lady Findlay had raised her handkerchief to her nose several times as well.

"Go ahead, sign and be quick about it," Da urged Logan. "We need to be on our way."

Rebellion pounded against Logan's ribs, and he thrust out his lower lip.

Something about this didn't feel right—made him slightly afraid and his tummy waffy.

Like when he awoke during the middle of the night and the castle was too quiet. Too ghostly and strange. And he lay alone in his chamber with only his sword and a carved dog for protection. Too scared to move or rise, but just as terrified to stay buried beneath the weighty bedcoverings.

"Why do *I* have to wed her? Why canna someone else?" Logan veered the fretting bairn another troubled glance and, leaning toward Da, whispered, "She's no' verra bonnie."

"Yer king asks it of ye, lad. As do I." Da indicated

where Logan should sign again.

So he must marry a strawberry-faced, drooling baby for a prissy king he'd never met?

Unfair!

Logan wasn't supposed to swear, but he could *think* oaths with no one the wiser. And right now, he wanted to think whole bunches of them.

Bloody hell. Blister and damn. God's toenails.

Bampot. Diddy. Scunner.

Shite. Shite. Shite!

What would Da do if Logan stomped his feet and hollered "Nae!" at the top of his voice or threw the quill on the floor, mashing it beneath his foot, cursing all the while?

If he was required to wed that red-faced bairn, shouldn't he have something in return like the adults?

Hmm...

Maybe...

"Can I have a puppy then?" Logan skewed a hopeful brow and chewed the side of his lower lip.

He really, *really* wanted a puppy, but Da always stalled, saying mayhap when he was older. And older never, ever—*ever*—came.

Logan squared his shoulders and jutted his chin. "If I be auld enough to become"—*what was the word?*—"be...trussed, then I'm auld enough to have my own dog."

Let Da argue against that.

"Be-trothed," Mr. Hyde muttered crossly beneath his breath, stressing each syllable. "The word is *Be. Trothed*. And the nerve of the lad. Askin' for a mongrel when he should be thankin' His Majesty for the honor he's bestowed upon the child."

Mr. Hyde shook his head and *tsked* reproachfully again.

Showed what the cranky old tosspot knew, comparing honor to a puppy. Lads didn't play with honor. Or have it curl up in their beds and keep them warm. Or lick their giggling faces until they gasped for air. Or keep them company in drafty, scary, old keeps.

Logan held his breath, afraid Da would say no. Again.

But this time, Da laughed, his smile folding his face clear to the corners in amusement, and even

Findlay's lips twitched a mite.

"Aye, ye can have yer puppy. Now sign the document. We need to depart soon if we're to make the first lodgin' house before nightfall." Da closed the dowry chest's lid and, after securing the lock, tucked the key into his sporran.

Logan murmured each of his five names, *Logan Greer Wallace Robert Rutherford,* as he laboriously wrote them, remembering to carefully shape the letters as his tutor demanded.

Only the nib scritching against the crisp parchment and the bairn's coos interrupted the eerie calm entombing the great hall.

A shiver juddered across his shoulders, and he hesitated.

"Go on. Ye're almost done." Da nudged his arm.

Once he'd finished, Mr. Hyde all but snatched the quill from Logan's hand and proceeded to scribble his name, sprinkle sand atop the ink, and, lastly, affix a fancy seal to the scarlet wax at the bottom.

"Can I play with Coburn now, Da?"

Beaming in a very pleased way Logan had never

seen before, his father dipped his square chin.

"As soon as ye say yer farewells and give the lass the gift ye brought, ye can play with yer cousin."

Logan opened his pouch and sticking his tongue between his teeth, fished around in his sporran for the pin. He'd assumed it was a present for Lady Findlay when Da asked him to carry the heart-shaped, crown-topped token.

Once he'd pulled the piece free, he turned it over and picked out a bit of fuzz—probably from his plaid—from the bright blue stone in the center.

"It matches her eyes." Palm upward, he extended the Luckenbooth brooch.

The bairn snatched it from his hand and promptly stuffed the scrolled end into her mouth. However, Lady Findlay gently took the clasp from her daughter at once.

"Nae, sweetin'. Ye'll hurt yerself."

Her voice sounded funny and tight, as if she tried not to cry. Her eyes looked strange too. Wide and watery and accusing.

Grabbing his wooden sword, Logan made to join

Coburn. Barely one year older and often mistaken for his twin, his cousin was also his best friend ever since Coburn came to live at the keep.

"Logan?" Lady Findlay's lyrical voice stopped him.

Holy rotten haddock.

What now?

Eager to find Coburn and slay all manner of mythical beasts from dragons to trows, Logan fingered the sword's smooth hilt and slowly faced her.

"M'lady?"

Her ladyship offered him a brave, if somewhat wobbly smile.

"I ken ye be young, and ye dinna fully understand what has transpired here today. But I ask ye to be kind to Mayra, to no' hurt her—to keep her from harm. And someday, perhaps, ye can come to love her. Can ye promise me that, Logan?"

After coming to stand before Lady Findlay, he cocked his head.

"Aye, m'lady. I surely can."

Bracing his hands on his upright sword, Logan

peered into the cradle.

Covered in lacy stuff, the infant gurgled, waved her chubby fists, and blinked her big blue eyes. Whitish bumps covered her face, and drool ran from one corner of her slobbery mouth.

Och.

He pinched his features tighter.

"Why's her face all puckered? And riddy and blotchy?" He touched his own smooth cheeks while eyeing her doubtfully. "Are ye sure the bairn is a lassie? She has nae hair."

Just like Mr. Hyde—bald as a stone or a goose egg.

"Aye, Mayra is a lass." Lady Findlay lifted the wee one from the cradle and, after arranging the bairn on her lap, brushed her fingers across the lass' head. "She's fair, like her father. It may take a while, but she'll have hair. Would ye like to hold her?"

Nae!

Logan shook his head and backed away. Horror of horrors. He'd rather cuddle a selkie or a kelpie. He never wanted to hold or touch the wriggling bairn.

Ever.

"I would have an oath from ye too, lad." Findlay went to one muscled knee before him, and still Logan had to crane his neck to meet the laird's eyes.

By jiminy, he's huge. Way bigger than Da.

"Court my wee lass beforehand," Findlay said. "And wait until she's passed her twentieth birthday to wed."

"Now see here," Mr. Hyde spluttered, his eyebrows writhing like great, giant, fuzzy, gray worms. "That's no' part of the settlement."

"Nae age nor courtship restrictions were specified, Hyde. Sloppy on yer part." Findlay's frigid smile nailed the nasty wee man to the hall's paneled wall. "If the lad likes, he can wait until he's in his fifth decade."

"We'll see what His Majesty has to say about that," sniffed the agent with a jerk of his head, sending another waft of foul odor from his person.

Dunrangour's laird leaned in and whispered in Logan's ear. "And when ye are an adult, and if ye dinna want to marry Mayra, petition the monarchy to

13

grant ye a reprieve. I shall ask too, if that's what ye want. But ye need to return her dowry else she canna marry another."

Logan veered a brief glance to the squirming infant. Not have to wed that blotchy-faced lass? Aye, that Logan could promise.

"Sir, it shall be as ye request."

Outside Glenliesh Village, Near Dunrangour Tower
12 March 1720

Mayra grinned at the days-old dun calves frolicking in the meadow, gleaming as if blanketed with enormous emeralds. Early-blooming Lady's Smock added faint lilac patches here and there. And if she weren't mistaken, a few bluebells already bobbed their cheerful heads amongst the green bordering the Windlespoons' estate.

The cold, wet winter seemed to drag on, each day longer than the previous. But at last, spring was almost upon the Highlands, and several shrubs and trees blossomed prematurely.

She wouldn't stop and say hello to her dearest

friend, Gaira, today. Gaira's doting parents had whisked her to Edinburgh for the Social Season, something Mayra would never experience.

Envy tried to jab her, but she resolutely tamped the dark sentiment down and focused on the lovely day instead.

As she expertly guided the dog cart along the muddy, rutted path still dotted with puddles from last night's blustery showers, Mayra smiled for the sheer joy of the sun's stroking rays and the vivid azure sky peeping between the ever-present silver-tinted clouds.

These were the days when she relished the Highlands; when spring promised new life, fresh hope, and possibly even a wee romping adventure.

Och, so wonderful, if only it might be so.

She detested the rain—almost a treasonous attitude for a Scot.

Yet the dampness, as well as everything cloaked in ugly grayish hues from palest ash to deepest charcoal—day after day, weeks on end—wore on her.

Especially since her only regular reprieve from the keep—also pewter-colored from its corbelling and crow-stepped gables to its corner turrets and bartizans—were these twice-weekly visits to the village.

Always—*always, God's teeth*—accompanied by someone.

Usually a clan member, one or two of her rapscallion teenage brothers, or Mayra's diligent middling-aged maid, Bettie. On rare occasions, dear Mum joined Mayra, but since Da had died two years ago, those instances had grown fewer and fewer.

The latter pairs' keen regard seldom left her longer than a minute, so seriously did they take her chaperonage. Consequently, nothing the least bit exciting ever occurred on the jaunts. Unless Mayra counted her brothers' penchant for regularly becoming embroiled in mischief of some sort in the village.

Today, Bettie sat in the dog cart's rear seat, food baskets for the needy tucked inside the rectangular box beneath her. She snored softly as Mayra skillfully guided Horace, their mild-tempered, going-to-fat gelding, along the well-worn, rutted path passing for a road.

No need to rush the horse. She'd delay her return as long as possible.

"I promised Maggi MacPherson I'd stop in for a short visit and share a pot of tea today after I deliver the baskets."

Mayra spared a swift glance behind her.

Chin drooping, Bettie dozed, her cream kerchief-covered head bouncing with each jar of the cart.

"Bettie?"

She stirred and blinked sleepily while yawning behind her hand.

"Do ye want to go with me, Bettie? Or would ye rather take a cup with yer sister, and I can collect ye afterward?"

"I'd like to see ye to the inn and then walk to Agnes', but I'm feelin' a wee bit waff." She sneezed and blinked watery eyes. "If ye promise no' to be more than a half an hour, Mayra, I suppose ye can see yerself there this one time. Straight to The Dozin' Stag and back, ye hear? Nae dawdlin' or givin' anyone cause to wag their tongue."

Did anyone ever need cause to blether?

Not in Mayra's limited experience.

"I dinna dawdle, as ye well ken. Besides, I canna imagine what could occur in such a short time that would raise even a single eyebrow hair."

Nothing exciting ever happened to Mayra. Ever.

"*Hmph.*" Bettie made a mollified sound before sneezing again. Her plum-round cheeks slightly flushed, she pulled her shawl snugger. "And let's be keepin' it that way, shall we?"

Arching an indignant brow, Mayra directed her attention back to the road as the neat village loomed ahead. Honestly, a little tittle-tattle on her behalf might prove most invigorating, given her wholly predictable and dull-as-a-worn-quill's life.

However, Bettie did appear a trifle peaked. Rather wan about her mouth too.

Swallowing her disappointment, Mayra released a slow sigh.

No loitering in the village today.

After she made her excuses to Maggi, she'd see Bettie home and to her bed as quickly as possible.

She'd take no chances with her beloved servant's health.

An hour later, having delivered food baskets to Widow Ainsley, the kind but dotty Pinkerton sisters, Dunrangour's deaf-as-a-turnip retired gardener, and four more to the kirk for other villagers in need, she drew the equipage before the MacPhersons' charming three-story lodging house.

Nearly a century of weather had worn the stone surface to a welcoming mellow, tawny-slate, a delightful contrast to the faded paint-chipped, poppy-red shutters.

As always, mouth-watering smells wafted from within, and Mayra's stomach gurgled in anticipation of enjoying one of Maggi MacPherson's Scotch pies. Mayra had skipped breakfast, and now she'd have to bear a hollow middle until she returned home.

Pressing a hand against her rumbling tummy, she squared her shoulders. More than one unfortunate villager dealt with hunger daily these past months. Assuredly, she could endure another hour or so.

"G'day, Miss Findlay."

A ready grin split Reed MacPherson's winter-pale face when Horace nudged his chest, demanding the boy rub his withers.

As the lad reached for the reins before obliging the persistent horse, she smiled.

Standing on his toes, Reed scratched Horace's coat just below his mane. "Ho, Horace. Ye like that, do ye?" Reed patted the gelding's side. "He's gettin' fatter, miss."

"Indeed, he is. Which is why it takes me so long to make the journey, though it's barely three miles. He's a lazy laddie, he is." She adjusted her *bergère* hat— sadly in need of a fresh ribbon—to a slightly jauntier angle. But how could she justify a new embellishment when villagers went without necessities? "I'll only be a few moments, Reed—just long enough to give yer mum my apologies. My abigail ails, and I must see her swiftly home."

"Aye, miss. I'll keep him company for ye. Saved him a carrot too."

Horace—his eyes half-closed in contentment— blew out a shuddery breath and bent his right leg. He'd not be pleased at having to turn right around and head for home. Too much exertion for one morning for the old boy.

"Ye spoil him, Reed."

Giving a soft laugh, Mayra stood. After pulling her wide skirt to the side, she prepared to descend the cart, a task she usually managed well without assistance, despite wearing panniers.

Searc MacPherson exited the inn with a man she'd never seen before. Hands behind his back and broad neck bent, Searc shook his head slowly at something the striking man said.

Just then, the stranger glanced upward and his arresting hazel eyes tangled with hers, jarring Mayra to her toes. And then he smiled—a dazzling flash of teeth in his tanned face.

In a twinkling, her mind went as blank as a sheet of fresh foolscap.

In a completely foreign fashion, she became all gangly limbs, caught her toe on her hem, and with a strangled squawk—somewhere between a crane's whoop and a sheep's bleat—toppled right off the cart.

Into his arms.

Oh, curdled custard.

Leaping forward, he'd somehow managed to close the distance in the blink of an eye. The alternative, being splayed on the ground in a wholly unladylike fashion, possibly injured, didn't bear contemplating.

She found herself clasped to a marvelous, solidly muscled chest while equally impressive firm arms cradled her shoulders and legs. The barest hint of mahogany whiskers shadowed the angular breadth of his neck and jaw—mere delicious inches away—and she forgot to breathe.

What a magnificent specimen of manhood. And he held her in his arms. Hopefully, he'd never let go.

Quite the most spectacular, fortunate accident ever to befall a maiden.

When her faulty lungs decided to function again, the most pleasant masculine scent filled her nostrils. Not a heavy fragrance, but a fresh, crisp, yet slightly musky scent—perhaps a hint of ale and tobacco too.

She inhaled a thorough, prolonged breath. Probably indecorous, that, although neither Mum nor

Bettie had ever specifically warned her against sniffing gentlemen amid their other rigid advice.

Who was he?

Why hadn't she seen him in Glenliesh before?

Perhaps he only traveled through their unremarkable hamlet?

Och, of course he did. The small village offered little in the way of entertainment or commerce.

Why did the thought cause such profound disappointment?

Mayra wasn't free to harbor romantic notions; not even in the most secret, most remote recesses of her mind. Well, fine, perhaps in the most clandestine, most isolated niches that even she daren't peek at except once or twice.

In the dark of night.

With her head buried beneath her thick coverlet.

From the *cuaran* boots enclosing the gentleman's feet to his nutmeg-colored jacket and dark blue waistcoat, the stranger's attire shouted quality. Hatless and tartan-free as he was, she couldn't hazard a guess as to his clan, or if he even boasted Scottish heritage at all.

Might he be a *Sassenach*?

A Frenchman?

Perhaps, but his vivid coloring implied Scots or Irish.

He cocked his russet head and his eyes, an unusual but enthralling shade between summer moss and toasted almonds, glinted merrily at her. An unhurried smile bent his strong lips, revealing a charming dimple in his left cheek and further crimping the corner of his twinkling eyes. From the creases also framing his strong, still upturned mouth, it appeared he smiled habitually.

Instead of mortification engulfing her—as would be appropriate—of its own accord, her mouth swept upward, accompanied by a wave of sheer and wholly foreign giddiness.

And by rumbledethumps, she, Mayra Effie Lilias Findlay, was not the giddy, gay, flibbertigibbet sort.

She didn't flirt or bat her eyes, or send secret messages to handsome gentlemen with her fan or gloves as Gaira was wont to do.

Perfectly content, Mayra made no effort to leave the blissful security of his arms, and he seemed disinclined to release her as well. And at five feet eight inches, she wasn't a wee sprite of a lass either. Yet his arms didn't tremble or shake with the exertion. In fact, she might've been a child, so effortlessly did he hold her.

Rather made her feel dainty and feminine.

And ever so naughty.

She peeked over his wide, sturdy shoulder.

Och and rot.

Bettie—Mum, as well—would cluck and fuss something awful when they learned a man had held her—in public too.

They would know soon enough, since a few villagers had seen her ungraceful tumble, and even now stood gawking at the attractive stranger in their midst.

The young ladies in particular seemed enthralled. They stared brazenly while striking provocative poses and thrusting their bosoms out, the whole while tittering about the *"braw mon"* with the wavy auburn hair.

How could Mayra blame them, when even though each scandalous moment she lingered in the *"braw mon's"* embrace heaped scoops of coal on the gossip fires, she couldn't bring herself to move an inch?

It wasn't every day a lass found herself in such a wonderfully awkward predicament.

Still, she ought to make some effort to leave his embrace.

Perhaps she'd contracted Bettie's ailment and fever had addled her reason.

Mayra touched her cheek, aware his startling, amused, greenish gaze trailed the movement.

Aye, verra warm.

That explained the languid heat encompassing her. Like warm honey trickled through her veins and turned her muscles to the consistency of hot-off-the-stove porridge.

And inarguably, no one had ever witnessed either warm honey or fresh porridge ever standing upright.

Finally clicking his gaping mouth closed, Searc

trundled to her, his apron strings flapping against his ample behind.

"Lass, I feared ye were about to take a nasty fall." He slapped the other man on his broad shoulder. "Good thing, our friend here is quicker on his feet than I am, aye?"

"Indeed. I'm most grateful." Must she sound so dafty and breathless? "Ye may put me down now, sir."

Or not.

I dinna mind stayin' in yer arms a trifle longer.

A week or so perhaps

As if he'd heard her, the handsome stranger's grasp firmed, pulling her minutely closer, his fingers pressing into the undersides of her thighs in a most thrilling way. A way that made her yearn to nestle closer, nuzzle his strong, delicious-smelling neck, and press her backside into his palms.

Another heady wave sluiced through her.

Was it her imagination, or did he seem almost as reluctant to release her as she was to have him set her down?

After he lowered her to the ground, one of his

hands lingered between her shoulder blades for a scrumptious, protracted moment. The heat penetrated her clothing, and she wouldn't be surprised when she disrobed tonight to find his palm imprinted on her back as if branded by his touch.

The urge to lean into his chest so overwhelmed her that she bit her lip.

What in Highland heather had come over her?

She'd been too shielded from young, devilishly attractive men, that was what. Other than family members, no male had ever embraced her. Good thing, too, if this was her doaty reaction.

Except...

Mayra doubted she'd respond like this with just any man.

A flush singed her already heated cheeks, and she set about righting her rumpled gown and lopsided hat, taking care to avoid the curious glances of the passersby. She must be above reproach, she well knew. Hadn't that been drilled into her over and over *and over* from the time she was a wee lass?

Aye, and Mayra always did what was expected of

her.

Nonetheless, mightn't a scandal be just the thing to put her betrothed off?

Would her intended then *finally* grant her request to end their arrangement?

Perhaps.

As the idea took root, she paused with her fussing.

Aye, an innocent flirtation *was* just the thing.

Och, and when word reached—

"May I ken whom I've had the pleasure of rescuin'?" Her hero raked a big hand through his gingerish locks, ruffling the curls atop his head.

Och. Bless Mayra's darned and mended stockings, Scots after all.

The way he said pleasure, the word rolling from his tongue in a low, mesmerizing brogue-turned-purr, wrenched her attention from her ministrations to his much-too-enticing lips.

Since when did a man's mouth fascinate her so?

That same mouth notched up a trifle before her gaze inched higher to lock with his.

Her heart frolicked about behind her ribs like a

litter of frisky kittens.

God help me.

A flirtation with this man might prove much too dangerous. Given her uncharacteristic, dazed response, *he* might be much too dangerous.

"Allow me to introduce ye." Searc beamed, his wide face wreathed in an enormous smile. "Miss Mayra Findlay, may I present Mr.—"

Searc scratched the back of his bulging neck, his face folded into confused creases. "I dinna recollect if I heard yer name when Mags registered ye."

Her hero dragged his attention from Mayra for an instant. "Och, aye...I'm...Coburn. Coburn Wallace."

As Mr. Wallace respectfully dipped his head, polite but not the least subservient, the sun caught the bronze streaks ribboning his russet hair.

"Mr. Coburn Wallace, Miss Mayra Findlay," Searc finished, another broad smile stretching his kind face, as if he'd been granted the highest honor in introducing them.

Mayra adjusted her sleeve, smoothing the slightly frayed cuff over her glove.

Och. No' done.

Searc only meant to be helpful, but in introducing her to the stranger, he overstepped propriety. Mum and Bettie wouldn't be pleased.

Mayra ought to nod her head and sweep past the men without another word. Most peculiar thing, however. Her feet stayed fixed where Mr. Wallace had deposited her and seemed as loath to move as Glen Coe's majestic mountains towering beyond the horizon.

"Miss Findlay? Of Dunrangour Tower?"

A different glint, keener and assessing rather than appreciative, entered Mr. Wallace's interesting eyes. His hot gaze leisurely crept to her scuffed half-boot clad feet and then made the reverse journey over her well-worn midnight-blue and hunter-green arisaid to rest on her hair secured in a simple knot beneath her hat.

"Aye, I am." Mayra's stomach renewed its frolicking when he'd said her name. Mindful of the intrigued onlookers, she inclined her head in what she hoped was a regal yet impersonal manner.

"May I ask what brings ye to our fair village, Mr. Wallace?"

2

Damn his eyes, Logan was in it to his raised brows now. And he detested trickery.

"I'm visitin' relatives after three years abroad, Miss Findlay."

Not exactly a lie, but enough of a deception that his conscience chafed worse than sliding across Loch Tolhorf's frozen surface.

Bare arsed.

More precisely, he'd left Lockelieth in outrage after falling out with his father upon learning Da had spent a great deal—*nearly all, truth be told*—of Miss Findlay's dowry entrusted to his care until she and Logan wed.

Blinded by his much younger wife's exotic beauty, Da had succumbed to Rodena's extravagant demands. In doing so, he'd forsworn his scruples, violated the settlement terms, and obligated Logan to honor the cursed troth.

Unless he paid back the monies. Monies he didn't possess.

That had spurred him to delve into a variety of risky business ventures while abroad, a few teetering on respectability's fringes, and none of which paid a quick return.

But then again, he'd believed he had at least another year to make his fortune before exchanging vows.

Only—*blast my damnable luck*—two months ago, he'd received word his father had fallen gravely ill. On the harried journey home, time and again Logan cursed himself for losing his temper and departing without telling Da farewell.

He'd arrived home mere days before his father died, leaving Logan an undisciplined clan, nigh on destitute serfs, a keep in deplorable condition, and empty estate coffers. Not to mention a widow more distraught about her future than her husband's death or the care of her young daughter, Isla.

For a fortnight after Da's death, Logan had prowled Lockelieth, half-pished in a grief-born fog, and later, a fury-born haze when he learned *all* of Mayra's dowry was now gone—squandered down to the last glistening pearl...on Rodena.

And that wasn't the worst hell-fired news.

Da had secretly mortgaged Lockelieth to her glorious ramparts and parapets with an impossibly large payment due by year's end.

A payment Logan had no means of making.

At present, Mayra's lands—lands Da claimed contained valuable ores—and the rest of her dowry were all that stood between Lockelieth and financial ruin.

More importantly, and the compelling reason he couldn't cancel the union with Mayra Findlay, Logan's people had suffered neglect these past few years as Da poured all his resources into Rodena's grasping, talon-tipped fingers.

Several clansmen murmured of dissent and rebellion so disillusioned were they by the plight

Father had brought upon them.

Logan's foreign business ventures had yet to produce a significant profit, and his only recourse was to convince Mayra to marry him before her twentieth birthday.

Much sooner, truth to tell.

Ideally, as quickly as arrangements could be made.

No legal writ forbade him from wedding her sooner, just a reluctant six-year-old lad's oath of honor.

He eyed her, chatting with the lad petting her well-fed horse. She was as likely to agree to the rushed union as sheep were to frolic about wearing periwigs, sniffing snuff, and sipping sherry.

"Are ye from near here, Mr. Wallace?"

Mayra picked a piece of straw from her plaid. Her endearing, not so subtle attempt to glean more information earned her an amused smile.

He'd piqued her interest.

Excellent.

Logan could almost see and hear her mind ticking off possibilities.

"I have family scattered hither and yon in Scotland and England. Even a few in the New World, Miss Findlay."

True enough.

Unlike the falsehood he'd told her about his identity.

The lie spilled from his mouth before he could consider another wiser, more honest option.

Coburn wouldn't be pleased when he learned of the ruse, and even less so when Logan asked him to keep his confidence regarding the matter. Despite his reputation with the ladies, Coburn's integrity made even the most devout saint appear a black-hearted sinner.

Nevertheless, and despite Logan's lie relegating him to the worst sort of knave, he didn't want Mayra to know he was her affianced just yet. Particularly since a stack of letters requesting an end to their betrothal sat neatly within in his desk's top drawer—an ever-present reminder of her disdain and reluctance.

That was one reason he'd chosen to stay in the village for the time being, rather than venture to

Dunrangour Tower directly. He was well within his rights to call on his intended, but he sought answers that he doubted he'd find at the keep.

After securing a room at The Dozing Stag for an undetermined length of time, Logan had exited the inn and spied a vision of such unexpected comeliness, his lungs stalled. And when his gaze collided with hers...

He knew.

Even before his attention locked on the Luckenbooth brooch, he *knew* she was Mayra Findlay—tall, fair, and blue-eyed like her sire, but with her mum's oval face, delicate bones, and bowed lips.

Never before had he experienced such a powerful and instant response to a woman.

And given her rosy cheeks and dazed expression, she'd been every bit as awestruck.

Either that or she was a promiscuous piece, practiced at snaring men with her guise of false innocence.

He skewed his mouth sideways a fraction.

How jaded and pessimistic he'd become, all because Da had married a wanton, only to learn her true character too late.

Not all women were cunning, manipulative bits like Rodena.

For the briefest instant—not more than a heartbeat really—Logan had almost told Mayra the truth. That this very day, *she* brought him to Glenliesh Village.

Or rather, seeking news of her had drawn him.

He'd opened his mouth to tell her, but unexpected and inexplicable fear of her reaction kept him mute.

What if her present fascination turned to contempt or scorn?

He still must wed her, willing or not, and he far preferred the former.

Instead, he'd held fast to his hastily-contrived plan: to poke around, and then contemplate his best course, depending on what he unearthed. He was fairly confident no one here would know of Coburn's kinship to him, so pretending to be his cousin shouldn't cause any issues.

Certainly, he didn't expect to encounter Mayra within an hour of arriving, nor could he have predicted his overwhelming reaction when he did. Even now, his jumbled thoughts caroused around in his mind, and his unruly member lay heavy and aching against his thigh.

Fine bloody time to don *Sassenach* garb.

A kilt would've saved him a great deal of mortification, but someone was sure to have recognized the Rutherford cerulean and scarlet plaid. Bending his knee and angling his leg forward, he prayed Mayra didn't notice his arousal, as he unwisely permitted himself another languid perusal of her.

Enchanting didn't begin to describe Mayra.

Even the freckles dotting her upturned nose, her faintly lopsided smile, and a small scar over her right eyebrow charmed in a precocious, elfin way. And she possessed the most unusual voice. Uncommonly low and rich for a woman, her husky brogue wrapped around his senses, bewitching and ensnaring him.

What did her laugh sound like?

Her cries of passion?

Deep and sultry like her voice?

Gettin' miles ahead of yerself there, auld chap.

Nevertheless, his manhood jerked in appreciation.

Damned intractable thing. Worse than an undisciplined pup.

Logan scrutinized her, trying to read her expression and gauge her thoughts.

No calculating or shrewdness shadowed Mayra's guileless blue gaze, and he relaxed the merest bit.

He'd stared into those wide eyes long ago, nearly two decades, before thick sable lashes framed them below winged, fawn-colored brows. His hungry gaze raked over her creamy skin, slightly turned up berry-pink mouth, dainty yet strong chin, and her hair.

Och, what magnificent hair.

The bald bairn now boasted a glorious halo of moon-spun tendrils, partially hidden beneath an atrocious straw hat with the ugliest—*what was that ghastly color?*—ribbon he'd ever seen. Her arisaid's bright hues complemented her coloring, unlike the simple woolen gown of an indistinguishable shade somewhere between tree bark and muddy riverbank brown.

She wasn't exactly attired in the first stare of fashion, yet she didn't seem ashamed or self-conscious of her clothing. Truthfully, he'd expected to find her wearing the finest English garments money could buy, as his stepmum was wont to do.

He angled his head and folded his arms.

That he recognized Mayra also flabbergasted him.

How many years since he'd last seen her?

Ten?

No, more.

The shy, awkward, rickle-a-bones lassie he'd last seen had blossomed into a rare and exquisite woman. After holding that tempting armful scant moments before, he almost hurled his plans into the tosspot.

What difference did it make if she knew who he was now?

She would soon enough in any event.

Roderick Findlay's words—words Logan hadn't recalled until this moment—echoed in his head.

"Court her."

3

L ogan angled his head. Why not?

He'd promised her father to woo her, hadn't he? A short courtship couldn't hurt, albeit he'd have to tell her who he was, and soon.

God's bones.

What if he succeeded in engaging her affections and she fell in love with him?

The Coburn me?

Now that would be one hell of a conundrum.

No, he wouldn't let it go that far.

To do so would be unjust and cruel. He'd be no better than Rodena. That truth gave him pause and turned his stomach sour.

He'd given Lady Findlay his word he'd not hurt Mayra, and Logan was a man of his word. Even if the oath had been given as a wee, confused lad who'd only coveted another sword fight with his cousin before he had to endure a tedious coach ride home.

A self-recriminating smile pulled Logan's mouth sideways once more.

Hadn't he also vowed—quite adamantly, as he recalled—he never wanted to touch Mayra?

Ever.

And he'd also promised to try to love her.

That sentiment had come full circle, and after embracing her lush form, he itched to touch—taste, caress, and kiss too—every last inch of her pearly skin, to run his fingers through her marvelous silky mane of hair, and sample her mouth that looked to have just eaten ripe raspberries.

Could those lips possibly taste as sweet as they appeared or her hair feel as soft as the glossy cloud atop her head promised?

Primal male satisfaction thrummed through him.

By Hades, she was already his.

His!

Until this moment, he'd refused to admit the fact

or, for that matter, acknowledge the distasteful, unwanted betrothal at all. Years ago, he'd managed to stuff the inconvenience into a grim corner of his mind and live his life as he pleased, more or less.

The awareness that he should've asked to have the agreement voided niggled the tattered edges of his conscience every now and again, and he'd always dismissed the task as an inconvenience he'd attend to later.

Except—*devil seize it*—he'd waited too damned long to petition the Crown.

And now...

A familiar tremor of frustrated anger prodded his gut.

Now, thanks to Da and that vain hellcat he married, Logan was stuck faster than an ant in cement.

Marry Mayra Findlay he would, regardless of where her affections or interests might lie.

He'd no choice. Too many people's wellbeing depended upon it. But, by Hades, he'd garner her true character beforehand and take precautions as needed if she proved to be something other than a virtuous woman.

Pointedly redirecting his melancholic musings, Logan turned his attention to the purpose of his visit—to learn as much as he could about his luscious intended.

"How, if I may be so bold as to ask, do ye ken of me?" Mayra's patient, expectant gaze held his.

No timid, retiring miss here, but neither, he'd vow, was she a flirt.

Aye, but appearances could be mightily deceptive, as he and Da—God rest his sorry soul—could attest.

Rodena's beautiful, haughty face popped to mind, ruining Logan's jovial mood again.

He'd not be cuckolded and humiliated—forced to acknowledge another man's seed as his offspring as Da had been.

Stupid, besotted old fool, falling under Rodena's spell.

In the end, her sluttish behavior, avariciousness, and cold, callous disregard strangled Da's affection and crushed his heart. No surprise he'd died of heart failure.

Suddenly weary, Logan passed a hand over his eyes.

Enough ruminating about that banshee when an angel stood before him.

Innocent interest filled Mayra's frank yet intelligent gaze, the color of the Highland's early morning summer sky.

He didn't detect a trace of coquetry or seduction, and he found her lack of guile all the more appealing. His betrothed wasn't a wanton, nor did she seem spoiled, as many pampered, high-born daughters were.

How to answer Mayra's question?

How *had* he heard of her?

She'd not be hearing the truth just yet.

He wasn't an idiot. He couldn't afford to frighten her off.

Precisely how peeved would she be when he told her who he really was?

He'd encountered her but five minutes ago, yet he'd wager her remaining dowry—the half the Findlays still held—she wasn't the type to overlook deceit, which made his situation all the more precarious.

Although he didn't want to take an infuriated lass

to wife, he must uncover what prompted her zealous and repeated—two-and-twenty at last count—requests to terminate their agreement.

To be fair, Mayra hadn't had any more say in the arrangement than Logan. But since he couldn't grant her plea and free her, he'd do his utmost to court her.

He wasn't foolish enough to suppose he might easily win her heart.

Her letters, polite and straightforward, clearly indicated she thought him a negligent, selfish, boorish jackanapes.

In a bothersome very brief time, he'd have to prove he wasn't.

But what about this mammoth lie?

Fine, prove he wasn't a complete and utter blackguard then.

Slamming the door on his musings, he gave her his most disarming smile.

She blinked as if momentarily stunned. Or was she unaccustomed to male attention?

Now that presented an interesting scenario.

"I seem to remember someone mentionin' ye in

connection with Dunrangour when I was in Edinburgh last month, Miss Findlay."

He scrambled to summon the name of an acquaintance they might have in common, but someone she wasn't intimate with if she asked who.

Instead of inquiring, however, her pretty mouth turned upward a trifle.

"My dearest friend, Gaira Windlespoon is to wed there in April. And my mum is accompanyin' me to the city for the ceremony. There's to be a masque ball. I've never attended a ball either."

Did the Findlays not entertain, then?

Melancholy and yearning colored her throaty voice. "I've heard it's a lovely city, and I've always wondered how different life is there from the Highlands."

"Edinburgh has many stunnin' features to be sure, but as with all highly-populated places, poverty and sanitation issues abound. I dinna mind visitin', but I'd never want to live there."

After three years, Logan was good and done with urban life, particularly filthy, malodorous port cities.

Mayra couldn't imagine town squalor, the stench or the impoverishment if she'd never seen or smelled them.

Fair brow furrowed in faint but noticeable lines, she swept the village a wistful glance.

"We've privation here as well, Mr. Wallace. In fact, that's why I came to town. To deliver food baskets. But now, I really must be off. My maid awaits me, and I've duties to attend to at home."

Times were tough for many, and word had it the Dunrangour didn't fare that much better than Lockelieth since Laird Roderick Findlay's death two years ago. That explained Mayra's humble attire, and yet she provided food to hungry villagers.

Had the Findlays been forced to tap into her remaining dowry? Perhaps that was why she was so insistent upon ending their betrothal.

What would happen to Lockelieth then?

What would happen to Mayra?

Dowerless, she wasn't likely to find another respectable offer.

Och, but she wasn't entirely dowerless, was she?

The land settled upon her was quite valuable.

Particularly if it contained copper and silver, as rumored.

A peely-wally sensation churned his gut.

It mattered not.

He couldn't release her.

Not without returning the other portion. The squandered share.

His honor wouldn't permit anything less, and aside from selling Lockelieth's acres, he had no way of doing so, and without land, the estate couldn't support itself.

Bloody fine impossible situation his father had left Logan to sort out.

Mayra gave MacPherson, intently watching their exchange, a cheery smile.

"Would ye please give yer wife my apologies? Bettie ails, and I must fetch her and see her home. Tell Maggi I promise to have tea when I return on Friday."

"Aye, lass. She'll be disappointed, I've nae doubt, but ye're wise to see Bettie to the keep. I'll tell my missus for ye now." He extended his palm to Logan, and the men shook hands. "It's welcome ye be to stay for as long as ye like, sir."

After shaking hands, he gestured to the skinny boy tending Mayra's horse. "As soon as Miss Findlay leaves, Reed, get yerself to the stables and help yer brother finish muckin' the stalls. Then both of ye come in and eat."

"Aye, Da." Reed shook his head, his overly-long shock of sandy hair flying about his neck as he rubbed the dozing horse's forehead.

With a polite, deferential dip of his head, MacPherson sauntered back into the inn.

Logan patted the boy's shoulder. "Ye go along, lad. I can assist Miss Findlay. I can hear yer stomach rumblin' from here."

"Thank ye, sir!" Reed bobbed his tousled head, giving them a gap-toothed grin. "Until Friday, Miss."

He tore to the stables, his scrawny legs churning.

Mayra's charming smile and the pink tinging her satiny cheeks suggested she wasn't opposed to Logan's assistance. Or else he'd quite forgotten how to read a woman's interest, and he hadn't been celibate *that* long, by God.

Taking her elbow, Logan guided her the few feet back to the cart.

"It was a pleasure to make yer acquaintance, Miss Findlay. I pray I might have the honor of seein' ye again."

4

Wicked of Logan to suggest it. To test Mayra. Without giving her any notion of his status or standing.

He couldn't decide which he wanted more—for her to politely defer and say she couldn't, or to eagerly agree.

Hesitation shadowed her features, as if she weren't certain how to respond. She brushed a stray strand of silky, flaxen hair behind her ear. Indecision warred with desire in her lovely eyes. She sensed the immediate attraction too, but if she were the innocent he hoped, unlike him, she wasn't sure precisely what she felt.

Mayra gazed at him with such intensity—innocence mixed with keen interest and perhaps more than a little uncertainty.

She disna ken who ye really are.

She would. And soon.

After all, he didn't have time to dawdle in an extended courtship. A month—two at most. For the time being, he'd pursue and enjoy this peculiar enchantment.

He well knew he might not like what he uncovered about Mayra Findlay, but he knew his duty too.

"May I help ye?" He canted his head toward the cart's seat while gesturing.

She searched his face and something deep within her eyes mellowed.

"Aye. Please."

In one adroit movement, Logan placed his hands around her trim waist and hoisted her onto the cart. His palms continued to tingle, wrist to fingertips, from the completely chaste contact.

"Thank ye, Mr. Wallace. I should like for us to meet again."

What would she propose?

Once settled on the seat, she accepted the reins he extended.

"I come to the village twice a week. Tuesday and Friday mornings, and I generally take tea at the inn with Mrs. MacPherson when I do."

Clever lass. She hadn't committed to seeing him, but she'd let him know her interest, all the while staying inside propriety's boundaries.

"I shall eagerly anticipate Friday's arrival then."

Giving him her fetching, slightly off-center smile, she clicked her tongue. "Walk on, Horace."

The portly gelding reluctantly ambled forward. Hands on his hips, Logan didn't move until the cart rattled around a corner.

Look back.

Just before Mayra disappeared, she cast a furtive glance over her shoulder, and he waved once.

Her lips tilted, but she didn't return the gesture.

Swinging to face the inn, he bumped into a passing matron.

Hell's bells and cockle shells.

"Logan, lad? Be that really ye?"

~*~

Two days later, the tension bunching Logan's shoulders eased as the drizzly dawn's metallic gray revealed a figure lounging, one knee raised, on a boulder beside Loch Tolhorf.

A horse grazed nearby, and fog drifted lazily upward from the ebony waters, shrouding all but the topmost limbs of the towering pines dotting the far shoreline.

Thank God.

Coburn had received Logan's message.

At Logan's approach, his cousin turned his head and pulled his tam lower over his ears, but he didn't bother rising.

"Pray tell me what was so urgent I had to freeze my ballocks off waitin' for ye in the dark at this ungodly hour, Logan? I had to ride most of the night to make it here on time."

A tiny vapor cloud accompanied each peeved, weary word. Coburn didn't like to be separated from his mattress, or whatever lass had warmed his bed, before the sun rose.

A grin threatened, but Logan wrestled it into submission. He needed his cousin's cooperation. Must have it, else his plan would evaporate as surely as the thick mist now hovering between the trees' trunks.

"I want to assure ye stay away from Glenliesh while I'm there." He absently stroked his mount's neck. "Actually, it might be better if ye left the area altogether for a while. Mayhap a trip to Edinburgh?"

He offered a cheery smile to offset his blunt suggestion.

Jacca, Logan's smoky cream gelding, snorted and stamped his feet, and Coburn adjusted his collar higher to block the bone-piercing breeze.

Aye, wretchedly brisk this morning.

Even with coat and plaid, frigid little toes scampered the length of Logan's spine, and a shudder shook him.

The cold dampness crept into the creases and crannies, and settled heavy and dank in a person's marrow, reluctant to leave even when one went indoors.

"And why, exactly, would I want to do any such thing, Cousin?" Coburn arched a smug brow.

Logan scratched his temple, tempering what he had to say with a hitched shoulder and a deliberate nonchalant mien. Coburn wasn't going to be pleased.

"I may have led the villagers and my betrothed to think that I'm ye."

His heart had dived to his boots and squirmed there, like weevils in porridge oats, several uncomfortable moments when he'd bumped into Lockelieth's former cook the other day.

How could he possibly have forgotten Annag Homles lived with her daughter in Glenliesh now? She might very well ruin his hastily contrived scheme.

For the clan's sake, Annag had promised to keep his secret, but unease nipped sharply, nonetheless.

As a child, he'd heard her blethering with the other servants, though never maliciously. He prayed loyalty would seal her lips. At least long enough to win Mayra's favor.

"May have? By chance? In passin'?" Coburn lurched to his feet, his eyes flint hard and angry as he glared at Logan. "Are ye off yer bloody head?"

"Nae." *No' completely, anyway.* "I'm just a fool who acted impulsively and didna control his tongue." Logan dismounted and explained his encounter with Mayra, leaving off his immediate, profound attraction and fascination.

His cousin wouldn't be able to resist roasting him. As it was suspicion that danced in his astute gaze.

"I want to discover why she's so desperate to end our betrothal, and after what Rodena did to Da, I dinna want any foul surprises when we're married."

Fishing around in his coat pocket, Coburn grumbled, "Ye're a damned, stupid imbecile. And what's more, it's no' like ye at all. In fact, ye despise charlatans and frauds. Anythin' remotely disreputable and ye distance yerself."

Everything Coburn said was usually true.

Coburn shook his head, puzzlement folding his brow. "Ye ken she'll be furious when ye tell her? And ye'd better hope to God she disna uncover the truth on her own."

"I've considered that possibility," Logan admitted.

"Which is why I asked ye to meet me here at this miserable hour."

Mouth pressed into a bitter line, Coburn shook his head. "Bloody glad I am that I'm no' ye."

"So ye've mentioned several times previously." Irony, dryer than burned toast, leeched into Logan's voice. Coburn had never envied his position. Logan suspected Coburn found the responsibility and duties too demanding and constraining. "I promise ye, if ye met her, ye'd think much differently."

"*Aahhh.*"

Coburn dragged the word out, his eyes fairly dancing with gloating amusement, his mouth quirked into a damned annoying grin.

"So it's like that, is it? She's grown into a beauty." He jabbed a finger toward Logan's chest. "And ye're itchin' to bed the lass. Explains a lot. Aye, it does indeed."

5

Logan donned a battle-scarred glower but choked off his immediate vulgar retort.

He found Mayra's keen wit every bit as attractive as her face and form—*well almost*—but he'd forsake whisky for a month before admitting any such thing to Coburn.

"I dinna ken if I want to make myself scarce." Rubbing his chin, Coburn tilted his head. "Maybe I want to see this lass that's caused ye to hurl aside yer common sense and act the moon-eyed swain."

"Go bugger yerself, Cousin." So much for controlling his temper.

Coburn's shout of laughter startled a large bird from its nest. The annoyed *ke-ke* identified a goshawk taking wing.

"Nae need. I have lasses standin' in line to warm my bed. And unlike ye, I occasionally"—*more often than no', Cousin*—"take advantage of their generous offers."

"Since I have nae desire to hear about yer latest romantic exploit, I'll be on my way. Mayra leaves for Edinburgh shortly. I'll send word when she does. Wouldna do for her to encounter ye there though— even if I have told her the whole of it by then." Logan raised a commanding brow. The one that told his cousin to hold his wheesht. Or else. "If I'm successful, we may have a weddin' date set by then too."

That didn't give him long to accomplish what he needed to. Mayra's twice-weekly trips to Glenliesh would have to suffice unless he found other opportunities to spend time with her.

But not at Dunrangour Tower while he still pretended to be Coburn Wallace.

Lady Findlay most definitely wouldn't approve or permit such outrageousness.

"Just a moment." Coburn finally withdrew a crumpled letter, then proceeded to try to smooth the deep creases. Extending the hopelessly wrinkled missive, he wiggled the paper, which crackled and rattled in protest.

"This came for ye yesterday. It's from yer Miss Findlay."

"Nae doubt another appeal to terminate our agreement."

Accepting the note, Logan grimaced, and after quickly glancing at her neat, feminine script, tucked the rectangle into his jacket. He wasn't about to read it with his grinning-like-an-imbecile cousin looking on.

He patted his chest. "I believe this makes three-and-twenty. She's persistent. I'll give her that."

Persistent. Intriguing. Beguiling.

Not what he expected at all. Although what he had anticipated, he couldn't quite define. His thoughts marching along those sentimental paths might prove worrisome, however.

Coburn angled his coppery head, his astute gaze probing. "And after ye've finished pokin' about, do ye intend to cry off if ye uncover somethin'...ah...untoward or unpleasant?"

If only Logan could have done so.

Heaving a gusty breath, he gave the merest negative shake of his head. "Nae, I canna. Ye ken Da spent part of the dowry, and I have nae way to repay it."

"Aye. I ken, Logan. But if ye're still keen on weddin' and beddin' the lass, why skulk around?"

Logan studied the Scots pines' angular forms ringing the loch's other side where a rare, brave moonbeam slashed the fog and tickled the water's glistening surface.

"Just a few more minutes, boy," Coburn patted his restless mount's withers.

Devil it.

Logan was loath to admit the ugly truth, even to the person he held dearest. Though he was obligated to marry Mayra, if she turned out to be a wanton harlot, he could at least refrain from giving her his heart, no matter how enticing her lips, mesmerizing her eyes, or alluring the rest of her luscious form.

"Well, Logan? I have a right to ken why ye're impersonatin' me. Particularly since my decorum, charm, taste in clothin', and appeal to the fairer sex far exceeds yers." Coburn gave him a rakish wink.

His cousin baited him, but Logan refused to take the lure.

"I'd like to ken what I'm in for beforehand," Logan said, matter of fact. "I winna be made a fool, an object of scorn and pity, like Da."

Head tilted, Coburn regarded Logan for an extended, contemplative moment.

"Fine. Ye can pretend to be me. And I'll keep my distance." Coburn's derisive smile revealed his grudging acquiescence. "But my advice, *my preference*, is that ye tell Miss Findlay the truth. And sooner rather than later. Deception's always a two-edged sword. And mark my words, Cousin, ye'll bitterly regret this sham."

A jot more tension dissolved, easing the tautness squeezing Logan's ribs.

He could always count on Coburn to have his back.

"Mayra's attendin' a weddin' in Edinburgh in April, and I hope to put things right long before then," he said, eyeing a red stag lurking at the forest's edge.

"Speakin' of Edinburgh," Coburn gathered his horse's reins, "Rodena took Isla and trundled off to her sister's there. A Lady Featherstone? Featherspoon? *Featherbrain?* Lady Feather Somebody-or-other, she claimed."

Good riddance.

Logan had wanted to send her packing for weeks, and only Isla prevented him from doing so.

"Did my stepmum abscond with the silver and anythin' else of worth she could steal?"

"Nae." Coburn shook his head and gave the cranky sky an equally cantankerous frown. "I had the servants watch her every move. She screeched and swore like a *hoore,* but in the end, she only took their clothin' and personal effects. Most wise of ye to lock the family jewels in the safe."

"Honestly, I expected all of the more valuable pieces to have been sold long ago. I suppose I owe that small reprieve to Rodena's greed and lust for glittery baubles." Logan rewrapped the wool scarf circling his neck.

Damned fickle weather. Worse than a popular courtesan.

"The poor, wee lass sobbed uncontrollably. She didna want to leave Lockelieth. Or ye." Coburn patted his restless stallion again.

Rodena ought to have left Isla at Lockelieth. The child would've been better off away from her sluttish mother.

Coburn swung into the saddle. "I havena been to Edinburgh in over a month. I'll go to town and see what mischief yer promiscuous stepmum embroils herself in. I'll admit to feelin' sorry for Isla. She's a sweet thing. Do ye ken yet who sired her?"

"Nae, and I doubt Rodena does either."

Logan scowled, relieved that his stepmum had departed but pity for her child nudged his conscience. "While ye're in town, would ye mind doin' a bit of research about silver and copper minin' in this region? Supposedly, there's a lode on the dowered parcel of Dunrangour's land. I'd like to ken if there's any basis to the rumor."

"Wouldna the locals be more likely to ken that?" Coburn scratched a bold eyebrow as another disgruntled bird took wing.

Logan inclined his head. "Possibly, but I'm guessin' official records would be kept in Edinburgh."

"Aye, I shall poke around." Coburn pressed his lips together, his countenance gone serious and stern. "Logan, dinna wait too long to tell Miss Findlay. A marriage begun with distrust and deceit likely winna improve in time."

Since when was his rakehell cousin an authority on the fairer sex?

Logan offered a twisted grin. "I ken ye're right. But I'm calf-deep in shite now. Nae help but to wade through it."

He, too, climbed into the saddle. "Coburn?"

Already picking his way along the rocky terrain, his cousin glanced up. "Aye?"

"Thank ye."

Coburn jostled his shoulders. "Ye're all I have left for kin, and I dinna want ye unhappy. Ye're an insufferable grouch when ye are." Affection crinkled the planes of his face and thickened his brogue.

"Send word if ye need me, Cousin, and I'll keep ye appraised of yer stepmum's activities."

6

Mayra cast an anxious eye to the sullen, armor-tinted sky and held the dog cart's reins with one hand while pulling her arisaid over her head with the other. She absently checked to assure the brooch securing the plaid rested in its designated place above her breasts.

"Get on with ye, Horace." She clicked her tongue.

The obstinate gelding flicked his ears back but ignored her prompting and continued his unhurried plodding.

By crackers, she'd have made better time astride a ram.

Sidesaddle.

"Come on. Go it!" She changed her tone to cajoling. "I'll give ye an extra portion of oats if ye pick up yer pace, sweet laddie. An apple too."

Maybe speaking to him in Scots would work.

Horace lazily glanced over his tawny shoulder, a distinct superior glint in his soft brandy-brown eyes, and barred his yellow teeth—*does he dare mock me?*—before facing forward and continuing his same sluggish gait.

A black slug *did* trot along swifter.

"Och, ye...ye stubborn, dafty...mule."

No ruder insult could she have hurled upon the gentle beast's head. She loved him, but he could be so very obstinate. And today of all days, she was in a terrible rush. For reasons other than the belligerent weather too.

The day after tomorrow she departed for Edinburgh, and she didn't know when she'd see Coburn again. Chances were, he'd not still be in the village when they returned at the end of April.

At the unwelcome truth, heaviness settled in her middle.

This was her fourth trip to the village since meeting him, and each prior time she'd encountered

Coburn, he'd given her a sigh-worthy smile, warm and inviting, as if he were as happy to see her as she was him.

And when he trailed his gaze over her, Mayra's flesh reacted in the most remarkable way—at once tingly and prickly, but also languid and melty.

She tipped her mouth sideways.

Was melty even a word?

Seated in The Dozing Stag's common room, like old friends, she and Coburn had chatted about all manner of polite, mundane things. She'd nibbled shortbread and sipped Maggi's special blend of tea while he savored a warm ale.

Her brothers, Bhric and Monroe, eager to visit village friends, left her to herself, either unaware of her rendezvous with Coburn or deeming them harmless in a public room.

When the time came to depart for home—always far too soon—Coburn had asked to walk Mayra to the village's edge, despite her brothers' certain curious gazes and mocking grins.

She'd wanted to agree but, nonetheless, prudence

dictated she decline his offer.

The lads would surely tell Mum, and that would be the end of any further outings.

Still, as faithful Horace had moseyed home, and her brothers good-naturedly ribbed one another or sang risqué ditties, she'd dared harbor secret thoughts.

Hopeful, fanciful, impossible, wonderful thoughts.

And today, she'd see Coburn again.

She gave a silent sigh, her mouth curved into a private smile. Her heart knocked against her ribs and her tummy quivered in anticipation. No, downright, well...giddiness.

Mayra hoped—oh, how she hoped!—providence favored her today.

A dreamy smile bent her mouth once more.

She'd never met anyone—more specifically, any toe-curling, nape-raising, stomach-tumbling man— quite like Coburn Wallace.

A charmer who, in an instant, made such a lasting and pulse-stuttering impression; she could yet recall his brilliant smile and the exciting sensation of his hands on her person. Never mind his intelligent, sable-lashed, mossy-green eyes, chestnut hair, glinting deep bronze where the sun caressed it, or his angular face— high cheekbones, chiseled chin, noble forehead.

His deep, lyrical voice, like melted chocolate— sweet and warm—mesmerized her from the instant she heard him laugh at something MacPherson said as they exited the inn.

In her mind, he'd become an incomparable. So very different than her darkling-tempered betrothed.

Another fretful survey of the irritable quicksilver heavens, Mayra puffed out her cheeks in frustration. Sure as chickens clucked, the portly, vicious-looking clouds were about to burst, and she'd be a sopped wretch by the time she made Glenliesh—guaranteeing her visit and the trip home would be utterly miserable.

And such unusual pains she'd taken with her appearance today too.

She wore one of her best gowns—a stretch, calling the three-year-old green-and-white striped garment such. She'd even dabbed a drop of her precious perfume behind each ear—her last gift from Da before he died.

Reaching beneath the soft plaid draped across her head, she patted her hair, then checked the pins and curls. Everything still felt in place. This new style—one which Gaira insisted was all the rage in Paris and London—seemed rather more trouble than it was worth. And, truth be told, appeared much more bird nest-like than a fashionable coiffure.

Mayra had spent hours on her toilette this morning, hence her delay in leaving the keep until afternoon. She feared moving her head too fast lest the whole tangle tumble loose and plop onto her shoulders.

If her head became wet, the carefully-arranged locks would droop faster than flower stems jammed into hot tea. She'd toddle into the village resembling one of the scruffy Highland cattle contentedly chewing their cuds in the adjacent field.

A sudden gust whisked past, ruffling the cattle's coats, and Mayra clapped her hand atop her head to hold the arisaid in place.

Perfectly lovely.

Couldn't favor shine upon her one blessed day?

A cow lifted her head, peering at Mayra through

the wavy veil covering her broad forehead. Looking cute with her wispy tangle of bangs, the beast slid her pink tongue out and licked her nose.

Another stiff breeze blew past, and a shiver pelted down the column of Mayra's spine faster than a mouse dashing to its hidey-hole. She shuddered again, and drew her plaid tighter around her shoulders.

Vanity—and trying to capture a certain man's attention and admiration—had her freezing her bum off.

Och, for certain she wouldn't mind having the cattle's thick, rain-repellent coats right now.

In the distance, the grouchy, chain mail-hued sky grumbled as thunderclouds billowed across the temperamental firmament. From the corner of her eye, she glimpsed a sudden blue flash.

Lightning too?

Why must the weather be so confounded uncooperative today? Today when she wanted to look her finest?

Despite the bitter weather, her spirit yet remained undaunted, for she made the trip to the village alone, and the new independence was glorious.

Only yesterday did Bettie finally feel well enough to leave her bed. Her accompanying Mayra today was out of the question. The boys—bless her horrid little brothers for being marvelous, mischievous whelps—were confined to their rooms for hiding their tutor's clothing.

Every last stitch.

And right before they were to depart the keep, Mum developed one of her wicked megrims. After taking headache powders and a hefty dose of laudanum, she'd taken to her bed.

Which meant—*joy of joys!*—after a great deal of finagling and convincing Mum that the poor, hungry souls in Glenliesh expected Mayra today, she bounced along on the dog cart by herself.

By myself, by Odin!

Not a grand escapade, but she'd cherish it nevertheless. She'd be perfectly safe on the short excursion without a clansman along to shadow her every move.

Sometimes, more often of late, Mayra simply

needed time alone. Needed to try new things; needed an adventure—to experience more of life outside Dunrangour Tower's massive walls.

Especially...

Heaving an audible sigh, she adjusted the reins, giving Horace more slack.

Especially if, despite all her attempts to the contrary, she wound up mistress of Lockelieth after all.

In just over a year.

She'd exchange one prison for another.

One oh-so-wretchedly-short year.

Mayra slumped on the padded seat until her stays pinched and forced her to sit upright again.

Nothing like ruminating about her neglectful intended, Logan Rutherford, to make a gloomy day even drearier. *That* albatross had hung around her neck since the first time a village boy winked at her, and she blushed and giggled with youthful pleasure.

She'd waved and given him a bashful smile.

Mum had wrapped an arm about Mayra's thin shoulders and, taking her aside, gently explained she was betrothed. Promised to a laird. And even at seven years old, she mustn't smile at or flirt with boys.

How does a wee lass flirt?

For that matter, how does an adult lass?

Did she dare try her hand today?

It couldn't be that difficult, could it?

No, but she'd not make a fool of herself, batting her lashes and puffing out her bosoms, all the while smiling coyly, as the village lasses had done that first day as they'd ogled Coburn.

Surely there were subtler, less forward means of showing a gentleman that he intrigued her. For instance, spending hours on the curls piled atop one's head.

In almost nineteen years, Mayra had no experience in the art of flirtation. Gaira had tried to teach her how to flirt with a fan and gloves, but Mayra had ended up in a fit of giggles with a broken fan.

Shielded from male attention and company, almost as if her parents feared she'd bring ruin upon herself, and therefore them, she confessed to a shy awkwardness around men.

Except for Coburn.

But she was betrothed, and therefore she needn't acquire the skill.

If Da hadn't stipulated she wait until her twentieth

birthday to wed, she might already call Lockelieth Keep home and Rutherford her husband.

Utterly appallin'.

Glee and excitement didn't cause her capering stomach's rolling this time, or the shudder rippling from shoulder to waist, like a dragon's giant, razor-tipped claws scraping her spine.

How many times had she begged her parents to end the troth? Too many to count.

However, until her strapping Da died from pneumonia, of all things, they'd adamantly maintained Rutherford must be the one to seek King George's permission to terminate the contract. And—curse him for being an uncaring, selfish churl—Logan Rutherford remained exasperatingly, annoyingly, infuriatingly silent on the matter.

Did he intend to ever speak to her?

Bah.

Why, for all the oats in Scotland, didn't he respond to their letters?

King William died six months after he'd insisted on the match between them. Surely King George would grant Rutherford's request to annul the contract if the obstinate man would only ask His Majesty.

And toward that end, Mayra had brazenly sent off another missive asking not only that Rutherford do so at his earliest convenience, but she'd also sent an epistle to King George, ever-so-politely requesting His Majesty to consider voiding the agreement as well.

What harm could come of it?

If the king denied her appeal, at least she'd have tried everything at her disposal, short of gamboling off to the colonies. She couldn't do it, of course. Leave Mum and the boys, perhaps never to see them or Scotland again.

Chin tucked to her chest to block the stinging wind, she gave an impish chuckle.

Horace flicked his ears and half-turned his head.

"I'm no' laughin' at ye, Horace. Just my foppish intended."

Wouldn't she have liked to see Logan Rutherford's arrogant face when he read that last part of her letter? Probably sent the prancing popinjay into a conniption. Had he needed his smelling salts to ward off the vapors?

She may have also hinted—rather strongly—to Rutherford that she'd prefer to wed someone who actually showed an interest in her.

A man who wasn't just taken with her dowry and land—a dowry that would've gone far to help support Dunrangour had Da permitted them to touch it.

He'd refused, saying Findlay honor forbade it.

Still, she'd prefer a man she could love. One who demonstrated common courtesy—for instance, answering letters or preventing lasses from potentially nasty tumbles.

Like a particular dashing auburn-haired Highlander with a rogue's smile and a rakish glint in his captivating eyes?

Eyes that one moment glowed like warm, dark honey edged with forest green, and the next, the browns and greens spiraled together. But eyes that always danced with a faintly seductive glint around the edges.

What color were Rutherford's eyes?

Squinting at Horace's wide, swaying behind, Mayra tried to recall.

Blue? Brown?

Devil red?

She hadn't seen him since she was seven, and all she recalled from that painful encounter as she peeked from behind Mum's skirts, was dark coppery hair above a benign, albeit bored countenance. Slender and tallish, he'd flicked a disinterested gaze over her as one might a piece of unappetizing fruit.

Mayra drew in a cleansing breath.

No sense stewing on her betrothal unpleasantness right now, for she fully intended to make the most of every single moment of freedom she had left.

If the king and Rutherford proved uncooperative.

Heaven help her if they did.

She wriggled the reins the teeniest bit.

"Come on, Horace. Please. I canna arrive lookin' like a selkie. No' today." Leaning forward a few inches, she confessed to the horse's broad back. "Coburn might be in the village again."

He simply must be.

Wicked of her to entertain such thoughts, but fanciful imaginations weren't actions. She knew her current status made her ineligible for suitors, but conversation was harmless, was it not? And she did so want to further her acquaintance with him even if naught could come of it.

Nothing outrageous or reproachful—

She straightened, going stiff for an instant.

Wait a devilish moment...

She'd harbored this thought before too.

Why, a scandal might be just the thing—the absolute perfect solution—to cause Logan Rutherford to call off the betrothal.

Mum had emphasized over and over—*and over*— that he loathed any hint of impropriety.

Eyes slightly narrowed, her mind churning, Mayra contemplated the feasibility.

Aye, it just might work.

Of course, she'd have to be cunning and cautious.

Verra, verra careful.

Her goal wasn't ruination, but simply to rid herself of an unwanted intended.

Still, her interest in Coburn was real. Disturbingly so. She'd best be vigilant in that regard too. He might prove to be a rapscallion or rake. A knave or reprobate, despite his overwhelming charm.

Mum and Bettie avowed men of that ilk were the hardest to trust, and a prudent woman wouldn't be so unwise. But how might Mayra discern the truth? She had pitiful, limited experience with men, and she couldn't exactly ask anyone outright.

Pardon me, but can ye tell me what ye ken of debonair Mr. Coburn Wallace?

Is he a womanizer, tippler, or given to gamblin'?

That would surely arch knowing, judgmental brows and send tongues to flapping faster than leaves during a spring storm, much like the one that threatened today. And, of course, it had lurked during the only trip in weeks where no pressing errands demanded Mayra's attention.

Except for the usual food deliveries and collecting a new length of ribbon for her hat, she was free to do what she wished for the afternoon. Mum insisted on the new hat trim, claiming Mayra was soon to be Lady Rutherford, and she couldn't go about looking beggarly.

If beggarly put off Logan Rutherford, Mayra would take to wearing her oldest gown and shoes. No, she'd go about barefoot with dirt between her toes.

Wasn't there a frayed cap in the rag bag? And a moth-eaten shawl too? Mayhap, she'd even smear a bit of earth or ashes on her chin and beneath her nails.

A grin split her face until Mum's and Bettie's horrified expressions intruded upon her humorous imaginings. They'd have apoplexy if she ambled about with a smudged face and soiled hands. Hard enough to explain wearing rags without having to justify a grimy countenance.

Nevertheless, the idea had merit.

A blustery gust slammed into her, and Horace's swishing tail indicated he found the weather as objectionable as she. A downpour would have him in a full-on sulk, and he might very well decline to tramp home.

It wouldn't be the first time the pigheaded beast refused to move his plump posterior, which is why he was one of the few remaining horses at Dunrangour.

Mayra quite anticipated a cup of steaming tea, a

cozy midday meal, and a long visit with Maggi MacPherson. Why, Mayra might spare an entire two or even three hours in the village if Coburn put in his usual appearance.

But everything depended on the feckless weather.

The air had gradually grown thicker and damper, and the sky had developed a peculiar greenish cast as the increasing wind tormented everything within its path.

Shivering, Mayra entreated Horace once more, appealing to the horse's preference for comfort.

"Ye do ken ye'll become soaked, and ye'll remain cold and wet 'til we arrive home?"

If they made it back to the keep this afternoon.

What she'd thought to be a typical bout of foul March weather looked to have developed into something much more serious.

To her delight, as if he understood he'd be subjected to a degree of discomfort, something the spoiled animal avoided at all costs, Horace broke into a slow trot.

Five minutes later, the heavens having been

merciful and refraining from dumping their contents on the already soggy Highlands, she tooled the vehicle along the village's main street. Upon spying a broad-shouldered, bronze-haired man striding into the lodging house, her heart beat faster, and she gave a tiny whoop of excitement.

Coburn.

8

Logan entered The Dozing Stag, sorely tempted to seek his chamber and indulge in a long nap. After another sleepless night and rising before dawn again today, sand scraped across his eyes each time he blinked his millstone-weighted eyelids.

Later returning to the village than he'd intended, his hours exploring the acreage Findlay dowered Mayra had proved most satisfying. Logan had found prime grazing lands, as well as several acres suitable for crops. A rocky crag, tunneling along the property's northern perimeter separating the dowered lands from the rest of Dunrangour's, needed further exploring too.

Da swore that particular piece contained copper and silver ores, though he never revealed how he'd come by the information.

Logan blinked drowsily, the movement sluggish and forced as he plowed his fingers through his thick hair in an effort to calm the wind-blown strands.

Head wooly from lack of sleep, he inclined his head at the smattering of patrons gawking to see who entered on such a blustery afternoon. A yawn escaped him as he scanned the common room.

No striking lass with moonlight gleaming in her silken hair, peaches tinting her cheeks, or summer's sky reflected in her winsome eyes sipped tea and nibbled shortbread.

By Odin, Mayra even had his musings waxing poetic. Must be the exhaustion causing the whimsical ramblings.

Had she come and gone already?

Disappointment, leaden and bitter, left a sour taste in his mouth.

He couldn't ask someone.

Too obvious.

Coburn was bloody right about him—he usually was, the irritating, confident arse.

Logan *was* an imbecile, caught neatly in his own trap.

This skulking around was unworthy of him and Mayra. Rash and stupid to not tell her his real identity. His ill-conceived impulse would make winning her more difficult. And each time they met and he continued the charade, it became harder to reveal the truth.

For God's sake, she was his betrothed.

He ought to ride straight to the keep and claim her this instant. Except, his innocent boyhood vow yet echoed in his guilty conscience, and her repeated requests to have their betrothal ended intrigued as much as puzzled.

Mayra's last troublesome letter raised the stakes treacherously high.

Perfectly impersonal politesse, nonetheless, her missive held a distinct accusatory tone and suggested his constant neglect surely indicated a lack of interest in pursuing their union. And therefore, it would *behoove*—her word—them to end the *farce*—again, her word—with the greatest of alacrity.

Where did she come up with her expansive vocabulary?

Exceptionally well-read for a female, it seemed.

And then, by Odin's gnarly pointed teeth, she'd neatly—he imagined the clever smile twitching her lovely, kissable mouth—dropped the lodestone.

Square on Logan's unsuspecting head.

Mayra had written King George too.

Saucy, brazen, unpredictable vixen.

Could things become any pricklier?

Why was she so frantic? So determined?

Arranged marriages were common enough, and this union strengthened both clans.

Not that he was altogether keen on the concept of marrying a woman he didn't know. But since he'd been backed into a corner, he might as well look on the favorable aspects.

Truth to tell, since encountering her, his opinion toward the match had warmed several degrees.

And her beauty and wit havena at all influenced ye?

Not to mention the swell of satiny breasts he'd glimpsed above her bodice when he'd held her that first day. Aye, any man still breathing—*dead too—*

93

would count himself fortunate to take such a bonnie lass to wife.

Nevertheless, Logan couldn't quite reconcile the amiable woman he saved to the resolute lass who'd presumed to write the king. Some might even accuse her of imprudence or impertinence.

Shaking his head once, he skewed his mouth into a half-appreciative, half-cynical grin.

Suggesting to Logan that he find *a more suitable bride*.

Damn, Mayra had a true Scotswoman's pluck and initiative. They were well-matched in that regard.

In other ways as well.

Namely, their mutual physical attraction, which multiplied each time he saw her.

His attention strayed outside—to the villagers rushing about, spearing fretful glances to the ominous sky—before he casually examined the men within the cozy taproom.

Had one of these men been Mayra's beau before he arrived in the village?

Something queer occurred behind his ribs, almost

like the time he'd fallen from a branch as a child. He couldn't find his breath as an excruciating vise squeezed his chest. All he could do was wait for the terrifying sensation to pass.

Only this feeling wasn't altogether terrifying—just unfamiliar and gut-wrenchingly uncomfortable. It spread thick, dark, and choking, like acrid smoke filling his lungs, stealing his breath, and muddling his reasoning.

He sucked in a long, stabilizing breath.

His imagination had him thinking gibberish.

Surely the sensation couldn't be possessiveness or jealousy.

Most assuredly no'.

He wasn't the jealous sort. At least...he hadn't been until now.

Until Mayra.

His eyelids half-lowered, Logan, nonetheless, examined each patron in turn.

Not a man present that he deemed worthy of his Mayra, and if any of these Scots were shy of their fortieth birthday, he'd gnaw his muddy, possibly manure-caked, boots.

According to MacPherson—the innkeeper had proved a ready wealth of information—Mayra was always well-chaperoned when she came to Glenliesh. And not only did she regularly give to the unfortunates, evidentially, her many attributes also included an acute intellect. She'd acted as Dunrangour's chief since her father's death, until her younger brother was old enough to succeed.

Oh, aye, his intended was quite an unexpectedly but delightfully complex woman.

Or...artfully deceptive.

Like Rodena?

The foul, unbidden sentiment wiggled its tenacious way into his contemplations.

Though MacPherson assured him Mayra was seldom out of her diligent chaperones' sights, Logan knew too well that loyal and devoted servants could be manipulated.

Particularly if they feared for their positions.

What type of a mistress was Mayra?

As kind and sweet as his first impression

indicated, or did she hide her true nature under false smiles and artificial demureness?

Rodena had.

Until she'd captured Da in her gossamer web, first sucking his integrity from him, bit by bit, and soon draining him of his joy, his pride, his money, and eventually, his will to live.

Livid didn't begin to describe his stepmum's reaction when Logan had cut off her funds.

A satisfied grin pulled his mouth upward as he wended his way between tables. No wonder she'd hied off to Edinburgh. However, he'd continue to provide for Isla, despite her questionable heritage. After all, the sweet, wee lass couldn't be faulted for her mum's infidelity, and she believed Da her father and Logan her brother.

Isla would never learn otherwise from him.

He wouldn't add cruelty to his growing list of sins.

Finding a secluded corner table, he dropped into the scratched chair and, after extending his legs, raised a forefinger and signaled MacPherson.

"A pint and strong tea if ye have it."

"Aye, Mr. Wallace." MacPherson's jowls trembled as he trundled to the bar. "Right away."

Logan's attention drifted to the activity outside once more. An odd yellow-green tint edged the pregnant clouds. Orange lightning flashed an angry, jagged streak moments before the heavens grumbled loudly.

Would Mayra come as promised?

God, he hoped so, for he longed to see her again, even if the desire was this side of selfish. But the petulant sky didn't bode well, and she was almost certainly guaranteed a thorough soaking, and perhaps pelting from hail as well if she dared the journey.

Far better for her to have remained at the keep in this weather.

In the days since they'd met, his mind had continually wound its way to pleasant musings about her. A few rather erotic daydreams too. That caused him no small amount of consternation.

In general, he didn't indulge in lewd imaginings about women.

For years, he'd ignored her—unforgivably—and

he shouldn't be a bit surprised that his inattention piqued her.

A great deal from the tenor of her letters. Self-recrimination battered his conscience. From the tone of her last note, she was ready to kick him head over arse or take a riding crop to him.

In his defense, he hadn't known of her many correspondences until he returned home.

Da confessed he'd been too distressed to forward them, afraid of Logan's reaction when he discovered Mayra was as opposed to the union as he. With the dowry spent, naught could be done now in any event.

Merely contemplating the ways her partial dowry might have benefited his clan caused unbidden ire to scuttle up his chest and close his throat.

With a weighty clunk, MacPherson set the tankard before Logan, foam dribbling over the pewter edge. A steaming cup of tea, a bowl of mutton stew, a plate with cold meats, cheese, sliced apples, and hard brown bread followed.

"Ye look like ye could use a bite." He wiped a dribble off the table. "My Maggi makes the best stew, she does. And she said ye missed breakin' yer fast again today."

Distinct curiosity rang in the last few words, but MacPherson wouldn't ask why Logan left the inn before light each morn. Though it was outwardly a respectable establishment, he wouldn't be shocked to learn a nefarious transaction or two took place beneath the inn's gabled roof on any given day.

"Thanks." Logan summoned a weary smile. "I appreciate it."

He wrapped a hand around the cup and promptly burned his fingertips. He blew on the tea before taking a tentative sip.

Hot and strong and plain. Just how he liked it.

Taking another drink, he relished the warmth seeping to his middle. He hadn't realized how chilled he'd become and welcomed the tea's soothing heat chasing the nip away.

The door swung open. A violent gust snatched the panel and slammed it against the wall.

9

Mrs. MacPherson uttered a startled squeak and wheeled toward the entrance, nearly dropping her full serving tray

Cheeks and nose glowing, and her hair a tousled mess, Mayra charged inside. After wrestling the door closed, she secured the latch and offered a weak, apologetic smile.

"I'm so sorry. The wind yanked the door right from my hands. I fear quite a storm is brewin'. I'm no' certain I'll be able to make it home."

"No' to worry, lass," Mrs. MacPherson assured her. "We've empty rooms. Lady Findlay would have my hide if I let ye even attempt such a thing. Did Reed see to auld Horace for ye?"

"Aye," Mayra affirmed with a husky chuckle.

"Horace actually trotted the last quarter-mile, so eager was he to reach the village. I dinna remember the last time the auld laddie moved so fast."

"Probably didna want to become wet." Mrs. MacPherson bustled to a table and unloaded the foaming tankards to a trio of old men hovering over a chessboard.

Vainly trying to secure the wayward spirally strands that had sprung loose from her coiffure, Mayra inspected the room. Her perusal halted when her bright azure gaze landed on Logan. A merry smile lit her eyes and tipped her mouth as she swept to him while removing her gloves.

Without waiting to be invited, she pulled out the chair opposite him and gracefully sank onto the seat. Her plaid and skirts billowed around her, and after plopping her rather worn gloves atop the equally well-used table, she continued to try to restore order to her hair.

Giving a small, abashed shrug, she explained. "I tried a new hairstyle. As ye can see, it didna fare well in the wind. At least I was spared that."

She pointed to the sheets of rain falling in torrents and lashing the windows.

Already, water had turned the street to mud and formed miniature rivers along its length.

"I think ye look lovely, even with yer hair tumblin' down. I've never seen such a fair-haired Scot before."

Indulging the urge to touch the shimmering tangles, Logan dared to flick a silvery curl teasing her shoulder.

Not wise.

A few patrons and Mrs. MacPherson watched him and Mayra with keen interest.

Arms raised, Mayra paused in taming her hair.

Her mouth parted, and her surprised but definitely pleased gaze scooted to his. Darker blue rimmed her irises today, possibly the effect of her pretty gown or her jovial mood.

"Ye, sir, are either a practiced liar, or a true gallant. For I caught a glimpse of myself in the window before I entered and this"—she pointed to her wild hair—"would cause the nag Cailleach to gnash her teeth in jealousy."

Mrs. MacPherson brushed the back of her hand across her brow. "Tea for ye, Miss Mayra? A Scotch pie too? I saved ye one."

"Och, Maggi. Ye're such a dear. Thank ye. I'm chilled through. And then would ye join us? If ye can spare a few minutes." Mayra gifted Mrs. MacPherson one of her brilliant smiles, and Logan's heart, or something in that vicinity, swelled with a joyful heat.

The minx had captivated him already.

How could that possibly be?

Mrs. MacPherson's curious gaze darted between Mayra and Logan.

No fool she.

"I'll fetch them for ye, and glad I'd be to rest my sore feet and enjoy a cup. Especially with a handsome young gentleman."

She winked and hurried away.

"I believe she's flirtin' with ye." Mayra chuckled, pushing one last pin into her hair. Winged brows peaked, she patted her head. "Do I look an absolute fright?"

"Nae such thing. Ye've managed to bring that bounty under control." Logan levered his fingers toward her head. "Is that yer hair's natural curl?"

He recalled her father's had been wavy, but nothing like the riot she'd just restrained.

"Aye, unfortunately," she agreed with a resigned nod. "And it gives me fits. Bettie too. Mum said I was bald as an egg until I was almost two, but when my hair did finally grow, it took on a life of its own."

He recollected well the bald bairn he'd thought was a lad. How he'd thought she wasn't bonnie.

She pulled a cute face. "I still remember them both tryin' to comb my tangles as a child. It took hours and hours. Or so it seemed."

He searched past her to the doorway. No cocky brothers or stern maid shadowed her today. "Didna Bettie accompany ye?"

"Nae, the poor dear's still recoverin', and my rascally brothers are confined to their chambers for hidin' their tutor's clothin'. Every last stitch, includin' his handkerchiefs and neckcloths. Mama says they're to have nothin' but gruel for the next three days, but I ken she'll forgive them before that."

Logan laughed and pulled his earlobe. He and Coburn had pulled a few antics like that with their unfortunate tutors too.

Unpinning the brooch holding her arisaid in place, Mayra cast him a saucy, sidelong look, her mouth curving into a proud smile. "I came to Glenliesh on my own today."

The brooch's familiar blue stone glinted faintly as she laid the plaid over the chair beside her. She'd worn the Luckenbooth brooch each time he'd seen her. As a testament to everyone that she was affianced?

Assuredly not the behavior of a *bint* or an immoral lass.

Clutching the table's edge with long, slender fingers, Mayra leaned forward, her sapphire eyes sparkling. My Laird, but she had the most expressive face and speaking eyes. A long wisp of hair she'd missed coiled across her nape.

"It's the first time. Ever. Can ye believe it? Me, nearly nineteen, and this is the only time I've been permitted the trip alone, even though Dunrangour is scarcely three miles away." Her gaze dropped to the table for a second. "I hope Mum will let me come by myself more often now."

He did too, for his time in the village must eventually come to an end, and he must win her over before it did. Before she left for Edinburgh and her friend's wedding.

All of his other attempts to arrange an encounter with her had met with failure. She was well and truly supervised.

Mayra gave a slightly disgusted, or perhaps frustrated, shake of her head.

"Do ye have any idea how annoyin' it is to be constantly chaperoned, Coburn? It's bad enough that we so seldom have visitors. At times, I feel we live in a different country, in a different time, for I have nae idea what happens elsewhere until months afterward."

Guarded so closely, no doubt she rarely spoke to a man alone, and yet the pleasure had been Logan's several times now. For whatever reason, for once, Fate seemed to have granted him favor.

He almost snorted aloud.

Was he actually giving Fate credit for any of this?

Fate, whom he'd blamed and cursed soundly for decades about his lot in life?

Mayra's enthusiasm over such a simple thing, being permitted a solitary trip to the village, both pleased and concerned him.

Had her life truly been so stark as a result of their mandated betrothal?

Why had her parents been overly strict?

Teasing the fringes of Logan's hazy memory of the day he'd become betrothed to Mayra, a dim image emerged of Mrs. Findlay softly weeping into her daughter's bundled chest while Roderick Findlay's warrior-fierce glowers burned holes through Da and that other oily little man.

Logan remembered next to nothing of the king's agent except his great, awful stench and big, yellow teeth. Like an oversized mountain hare. Enough to give a child nightmares.

Aye, the Findlays hadn't been enthusiastic about the arrangement, and who could blame them? They'd been forced to sacrifice their firstborn and, as it turned out, only daughter to a monarch's momentary fancy.

Da had never revealed why the king ordered the union. But given Mayra had been kept on a short tether, attended constantly and allowed few of the social privileges a gently-bred woman was generally permitted, her parents must have been threatened with something calamitous to cause them to take such extremes. Extremes still in place and enforced after Findlay's death.

A pang burgeoned, stabbing and burning in Logan's chest.

He'd never considered Mayra's plight in the arrangement, only selfishly rebelled at his life having been manipulated by others.

Logan despised being a human pawn and so, too, must she. And yet, wasn't he guilty as sin of doing the same thing this very moment by not being forthcoming?

Mayra touched her forefinger and thumb to the dainty pearl earbobs hanging from each delicate earlobe, checking the small gold clasps. "I do love comin' to town, and I'm so lookin' forward to

Edinburgh. We leave the day after tomorrow."

The day after tomorrow?

Damnation.

He wasn't ready to reveal the truth just yet.

Still, Logan had reason to be optimistic. His theory about Mayra possibly having a beau? Ground to powdery crumbs, and he couldn't be happier he was wrong.

No woman so thrilled about a solitary sojourn to town carried on illicit assignations.

Ridiculously pleased at his conclusion, Logan lifted the tankard and halted his burgeoning smile by taking a swig.

"And when will ye return?" He'd use the time to look visit Dunrangour Tower and explore that intriguing stretch of land supposedly hiding precious metals.

"Mum hasna said for certain, but I imagine it will be toward the end of April."

That bloody long?

He didn't have that much time to wait.

A contented sigh lifted Mayra's pert bosom, and

giving a little wave, she smiled at an elderly man, half-asleep and smoking a pipe before the roaring stone fireplace. "He was our gardener until we couldna afford—"

Catching her blunder, she stopped abruptly. Pink tinted her cheeks, and she fiddled with her gloves, straightening the fingertips.

So, the tattle of Dunrangour's financial woes was true.

That concerned Logan more than a little. Nevertheless, he changed the subject to avert her discomfort.

"That's an unusual clasp." He flicked a finger at the pin.

Would she tell him the truth of it? Why did her integrity matter when he was an unconscionable cur who was lying to her?

Her attention followed his movements, and the joy drained from her face as her thick lashes fluttered closed for a fraction.

"It's...it was a gift to me when I was verra small. Mum insists I wear it."

Slowly, she lifted her eyes, hesitation and resolution reflected there and obvious in her partially-raised chin.

"Mr. Wallace—"

"Call me Coburn, please."

She sent a harried glance around the room and bent farther over, her bosom brushing the table's worn edge.

Lucky piece of furniture.

Cool hardness crept into her wisp of a voice and pleated the corners of her narrowed eyes.

"Coburn, I think ye should ken. As an infant, I was promised in marriage."

10

As the rain turned to hail, pelting the sodden earth with minuscule white cannon balls, Mayra held her breath and squeezed the table's rough edge until her knuckles turned white.

Every muscle taut, she awaited Coburn's response.

What would he say?

Would distaste or annoyance darken his mossy eyes and turn his handsome mouth down?

Would he care at all?

Had she presumed his attraction to her more than it actually was?

Or—*curses*—did his roguish, oh-so-charming demeanor hide a knave's heart and morals after all? In which case, she may have dived from a sizzling pan straight into the fire's flames.

Nae. Nae.

Coburn was a good man.

An honorable man.

She could see it in his candid gaze. More than that, she sensed it in her spirit.

Mayra had seriously considered lying, but in the end, Coburn must be made aware of her betrothal. Most everyone in the village knew, and if he hadn't heard already, he soon would.

He must also know she was determined to end the inconvenience.

Silly though it might be, she couldn't bear for him to think ill of her, to believe her dishonest or deceptive when Logan Rutherford's regard meant less to her than that little brown spider tending its web in the window's corner.

True, she scarcely knew Coburn, but something had transpired between them when he held her in his burly arms and had deepened with each mesmerizing encounter since.

Something wonderful. And frightening. And unexplainable.

Yet, something that also made her want more from life and even more resolute to escape the bondage she had lived with almost since birth. To dare to pursue a different path, understanding fully the consequences of her bold choice.

Was she brave enough to take that course? To face the outcome, good or bad? Pushing her shoulders back, she gave a bold inward nod.

Aye, but mayhap not as much brave as desperate and unyielding.

A puppet she'd be no more.

If the king didn't grant her request—if he even bothered to read her missive, since a Highland lass from an obscure clan was wholly insignificant to His Majesty—then Rutherford must be forced to cry off.

Almost seventeen, her eldest brother, Bhric, was the same age as Mayra had been when Da died and she took over as Dunrangour's temporary laird.

Past time Bhric assumed his birthright, and with Mayra's dowry, the growing herd of Highland cattle, and the valuable lands returned to Dunrangour's estate, Mum and the lads should be fine.

Coburn's large fingers, the nails clean and square, encircled his mug as he lifted it to his mouth. A shock of mahogany hair fell across his forehead, and he swept it back into place with his other hand, revealing a faded, whitish scar along the outside of his palm.

A childhood wound perchance?

She still knew little about him, except that he had the most musical Scots brogue and his smoldering eyes...she became lost each time she looked into their mesmerizing depths.

Nevertheless, the unidentifiable feeling that took root in her soul days ago continued to blossom and grow. So startling and rapidly, it quite took her breath away. Either she was smitten or deranged for entertaining the thoughts and desires he—an enthralling and striking stranger—had aroused.

He wore *Sassenach* clothing again today. She quite liked his dark tobacco-brown jacket. It emphasized his wide shoulders and brought out the brownish flecks in his eyes.

He'd never mentioned what clan he called kin.

"Do ye ken him? The *mon* ye're supposed to

wed?" After tearing off a piece of bread, Logan popped it into his mouth.

She gave a short nod and shivered when the angry wind-born hail pummeled the window and a draft whisked over her, raising her flesh from neck to waist. Or did premonition make her fine nape hairs tingle?

"By that if ye mean, have I met him?" she asked. "Aye, I met him. Many years ago. But…I'm doin' my utmost to have the agreement nullified. I winna willingly marry a *mon* I only remember meetin' but once in almost nineteen years. A *mon* whose only interest, as far as I can discern, is my dowry and land. He winna even answer my letters. No' one."

Coburn swallowed and patted his mouth with his serviette, his manner hesitant. Or was that reservation making his features taut?

"I'd like to call him a fool and condemn his thoughtlessness, but is it possible, Mayra, he didna receive them?"

At the intensity in his arresting eyes, she paused, then frowned at the rumpled lace edging her bosom.

Could she possibly appear any more disheveled and dowdy?

She straightened the scrap and inclined her head.

"I suppose so, but no' likely. I've sent more than twenty over the course of three years. Da sent others. I have nae idea how many. And that still disna excuse the younger Rutherford ignorin' me. Da said Rutherford agreed to court me or would ask to have the agreement voided. He's done neither."

A six-year-old lad agreed to those terms, her conscience admonished.

"Ignorin' ye is unconscionable, I'll admit. If he kent the beautiful, fascinatin', intriguin' woman sittin' opposite me this instant, trust me, he'd count himself a thousand times a fool."

Condemnation seeped into Coburn's voice as he fingered his knife handle.

Mayra almost missed the last part of what he said, having grown deliciously hot to her toes when he called her beautiful, fascinating, and intriguing.

Did he truly think so?

For he but echoed her thoughts about him.

Searching his handsome face, she examined each plane, every angle; the seductive dimple so quick to appear; his strong, chiseled jaw covered with that smattering of russet stubble she longed to brush her cheek against; his brow with its three narrow furrows; the crinkling at the corners of his eyes; and finally, his full, tempting mouth.

Coburn gently probed. "What will ye do, Mayra, if he refuses to release ye? He may have reasons ye ken no' of."

She lifted a shoulder. "I've written His Majesty as well, and I've decided upon a rather reckless course, if I'm forced to go that far. I ken verra little of my affianced, other than the lasses sigh over him, and I've heard he's rather a stickler for propriety."

"He is, is he?" He seemed doubtful.

She crinkled her nose and brushed her fingers across her sleeve. "Any whisper of unseemliness or scandal, and he sniffs disdainfully, points his pompous nose in the air, and marches away, stiff-arsed."

Coburn choked and slapped his serviette over his face, coughing into it. Eyes watering, he managed to sputter, "Stiff-arsed?"

Mayra grinned and leaned low over the table once more.

"Och, aye. Like a poker's been rammed up his— *erm*...well, ye take my meanin'. Rutherford's verra pretentious. Plucks his brows, paints his face—pox scars, ye ken."

She nodded knowingly, just keeping her lips from twitching.

"He sniffs snuff. His hideous wigs are said to harbor vermin—the tiny, creepy-crawly kind, and he wears gallons and gallons of scent, 'cause he disna bathe except twice a year."

She shuddered delicately and pinched her nose in mock horror.

Coburn's shout of laughter drew the other common room occupants' attention, and they smiled when he continued to laugh into his hand. Shoulders shaking, he shook his head and swiped the corners of his eyes.

"Good God. Nae wonder ye didna want to marry the sot. He sounds repulsive as the devil himself." Mirth still twinkling his eyes, he swiped the corner of one with his knuckle again. "If ye've never been outside Glenliesh, how do ye ken so much about him?"

120

11

Giving him an impish grin, she leaned back in her chair and crossed her arms.

"I made all that up. Except the part about scandals. That much is true. The other is how I imagine him to be. He probably screams and jumps on a table when he sees a mouse or a toad too"

"Undoubtedly. Likely he swoons and requires smellin' salts if he encounters an adder or a spider."

"Indeed."

Coburn pushed his food aside, and leaned back in his chair, hooking an ankle over his knee.

She offered Maggi a bright smile as the woman bustled to their table and whispered out the side of her mouth to Coburn, "I'd rather nae speak of him with Maggi here."

"Wise, I think."

Wouldn't do to have the curious servant be privy to their intimate conversation. And Maggi would never broach Mayra's betrothal, fully aware the subject distressed her.

Maggi set tea and a fresh Scotch pie—the pastry lightly browned, flaky, and scrumptious-smelling—in front of Mayra, then placed another cup before the empty chair beside her. The chair scraped as Maggi pulled it from the table, and once she'd plopped onto the seat and scooted it forward, she heaved a great sigh.

"I can only spare ye a few minutes. Since my Caronwyn married, I've been runnin' my tail feathers off, I have." She dabbed at her damp forehead. "She was a huge help with the cookin' and cleanin'. 'Specially the dishes."

Mayra and Maggi jerked when thunder boomed loudly overhead, shaking the inn's rafters.

"Foul as foul can be outdoors today," Maggie sad.

Hail littered the mucky lane, and the afternoon sky, heavy with churning clouds occasionally lit with streaks of jagged lightning, sent long shadows into the inn. Two shingles blew off the blacksmith's roof a block down the street as the wind whistled and pounded against the common room's window panes.

Mayra took a sip of bracing tea, welcoming the warmth spreading from her stomach, soothing her frayed nerves. Her first time to town on her own and the worst spring storm in years descends.

Only an idiot would attempt to cross the street, let alone try to reach Dunrangour Tower in this.

All was not dismal, however.

Now, she had a legitimate excuse to linger with Coburn.

From the looks of the tempest, she might truly be forced to accept the MacPhersons' hospitality for the night. She hadn't funds with her to pay them, but she could send payment later. She'd not impose upon their generosity.

Pretending to adjust her serviette upon her lap, she observed Coburn chatting with Maggi.

He caught Mayra's subtle perusal and an enigmatic smile arced his lips.

Hours and hours of Coburn's pleasant company.

She couldn't imagine anything she'd prefer more.

"Please congratulate Caronwyn for us. I have a small gift from Mum and me." Mayra bent and collected a brown paper-wrapped package. "It's no' much, just embroidered handkerchiefs, and a crocheted doily."

"Ye and Lady Findlay needna have done that, Miss Mayra." Maggi accepted the gift with a grateful smile.

Plunking four irregular lumps of brown sugar into her cup, she gave Coburn the gimlet eye. As she stirred her tea, Maggi angled her head and continued to study him.

"Mr. Wallace, ye remind me of someone. I canna put my finger on who, but there's somethin' about yer eyes."

Coburn winked and dipped his spoon into his stew. "It's admiration for ye and yer fine cookin', Mrs. MacPherson." He tasted the soup and sighed dramatically. "Why, if ye werena already married, I'd go down on one knee this verra moment."

Color blossomed on Maggi's cheeks, and she fluttered her work-reddened fingers at him. "Oh, pish posh. Ye're a born charmer, ye rogue."

"What's this? Wallace, be ye flirtin' with my darlin' Mags?" Searc approached, wiping his hand on a towel. He gave his wife's shoulder a gentle squeeze. "My dear, I'm afeared the bread's burnin'."

"Och. I plum forgot. My mind's gone to puddin', it has." Maggi, as slender as her husband was round, sprang from her chair so quickly it would've toppled if he hadn't grabbed the back.

"Do either of ye need anythin' else?" MacPherson cast a worried eye to the nearly deserted street as the last of his regular patrons dared the hostile elements in order to reach their homes before the gale's full fury.

Only a young couple with a small child and two middling-aged gentlemen—one who looked to be a cleric—remained. Likely overnight guests or travelers unwilling to brave the storm's wrath.

"I'm perfectly content for now, but thank ye." Mayra took a dainty bite of her pie. "As always, the best I've ever eaten. Someday, I'll have Maggi's recipe from her."

Had Coburn seen the innkeeper's pensive glance at his nearly empty establishment?

"I'm fine, as well."

"I want to make sure my lads have the stock and stable secure. This looks to be a fierce storm." MacPherson threw the towel over his beefy shoulder, frowning as a gust slammed into the inn, rattling the windows and sending the walls to trembling. "Miss Findlay, ye canna return home in this. It's near dark as dusk already, and ye have the forest to travel through."

Despite the uncertainty marring her forehead, Mayra gave him a reassuring smile. "I ken. Maggi graciously said I might stay until the tempest passes. I'll have to send payment for the room later. I hope ye dinna mind. I dinna have more than a few shillings with me. I do hope Mum disna fret too much though. But I ken she'd prefer I remain here where it's safe than try to reach home in this squall."

"Ye needna worry about payment lass, and yer mum would want ye to stay. I best check on the stables." With a slight nod, MacPherson scuttled to the kitchen.

Lower lip clamped between her teeth and brows

knitted, Mayra peered outside. "Do ye think I might try to make it home? Mum will fuss somethin' awful if I dinna, and she mightna let me ever come to town again on my own."

Assuredly she wouldn't. And besides, Mayra loathed spending money on a chamber when a perfectly comfortable bed awaited her at Dunrangour.

Lifting her head, her gaze landed on the two armchairs before the hearth.

A slow smile bent her mouth.

She needn't accept a room from the MacPhersons at all. She could wait out the storm before the fire.

Coburn laid his palm atop Mayra's, yanking her attention to him—to his big tan hand covering hers. "I think she'd want ye to be safe most of all. But if ye're really worried, I shall take ye."

The shrieking gale attacked the shutters, hammering them violently against the inn, and a wooden bucket hurtled down the street, bouncing end over end.

"Nae. Searc's right. Trees could crash down. I think it wisest to stay here."

Her gaze sank again to his hand still resting upon

hers. Fine bronze hairs covered the knuckles and back.

"Coburn, I think I may have conceived a way to rid myself of Rutherford."

Did she dare tell him her reckless plan?

She barely knew him—*really knew him*—so why did she trust him so completely? Feel like she could share anything, and he'd understand?

Well, almost anything. Certainly not her blush-worthy musings regarding him.

Coburn spread her fingers, lacing his with hers, and tipped his mouth upward, the seductive curve lighting his handsome face and turning her joints to jelly.

Mayra ought to pull away, but all thought of doing so vanished when he started rubbing his rough thumb slowly over the back of her hand. She couldn't tear her eyes from the simple yet intimate, hypnotic movement.

The rest of the room, the other occupants, faded into a distant haze, until it was only she and Coburn.

"I ken ye feel this between us, Mayra. It's too powerful to disregard. I think we've stumbled onto somethin' rare. So beautiful and precious, we mustna ignore it."

Aye, impossible to ignore.

The desire and warmth in his rich, deep voice paled to the heat sparking in his hooded eyes.

Her nipples puckered in answer to the longing shimmering in his molten gaze.

Coburn raised her hand and brushed his lips across her knuckles in a swift, hot kiss, and an electric jolt raced up her arm.

Breathless, caught up in the moment, she didn't care if anyone noticed.

"Aye, it defies understandin' because this gift came upon us so swiftly, but it's real. Tell me ye dinna feel it too, my bonnie Mayra."

"Aye, but I dinna understand it," she shyly confessed. "We've only met these few times. I ken nothin' about ye."

Still she didn't withdraw her hand. Instead, Mayra turned hers over so that their palms met, and her fingers—*the strumpets*—curled into his in the most natural clasp.

The knowledge he felt the same irresistible, irrational draw enveloped her in comfort and confidence.

And hope. Real, genuine, viable hope.

For the first time, she dared contemplate loving someone.

Coburn strayed his forefinger to her wrist, tracing a narrow, sensuous path.

She bit her lip when little sparks zipped along her nerves. How she wanted him to move higher, to trail his fingers up her arms, over the span of her neck...

Perhaps—heavens, her thoughts ran along a naughty path—brush the swell above her bodice.

"I have a solution too." He firmed his grasp on her hand, his eyes now a deep, mesmerizing forest green.

Did desire turn them that color?

Desire for her?

She wrenched her wayward attention back to what he'd said. "Solution?"

To what?

Och, aye, Logan Rutherford.

"Ye could marry me, Mayra. As soon as the storm passes, we could find a rector. In fact, I think that *mon* yonder," he jutted his head toward the quiet chap, "might be a cleric."

12

Mayra's breath stalled.

No wink or mocking smile accompanied Coburn's extraordinary statement.

What a scrumptious, novel solution, even if he did but jest.

Quite the most perfect, insane, absurd, and oh-so-tempting idea she'd heard in a great, great while.

Ever, truth be told.

But entirely impossible. Impractical. Unfeasible. *Dangerous.*

Even had he been serious, the risk was simply too vast.

To have Dunrangour, everything the Findlays owned, forfeited to the Crown and face imprisonment or worse?

Nae. Nae. Imprudent at best and catastrophic at worst.

She knew full well why Da and Mum had agreed to the union between her and Rutherford. They'd told her plainly, because they wanted her to know just how callous and treacherous her future father-in-law was, so she'd never ever trust the scunner.

She squeezed Coburn's broad, strong fingertips between hers. "I ken ye're teasin', Coburn. I'm sure ye've nae more desire than I to bring a monarch's wrath upon yer family or mine by defyin' a king's edict."

"Wrath? Surely nothin' so verra severe." His fingers continued to work their seductive magic.

For certain, wantonness flowed in her veins if she responded like this to the mere touch of his hand upon hers.

"Ye think no', Coburn?"

Her gaze riveted on their interlaced fingers, she debated whether to tell him all.

Why not?

And she could also discover whether he counted

the Rutherfords as friends. May a goose nip her bum if he did, for he'd not like what she had to say.

"Are ye acquainted with the Rutherfords of Lockelieth Keep?"

"Aye. I ken of them. Artair Rutherford died recently." Head canted, Coburn regarded her, his mien suddenly more reserved.

Mayra's jaw sagged, her spine going rigid.

"He did? His son, Logan, is my betrothed. How could we no' have heard?"

"It takes some families longer than others to talk about great loss, and ye've admitted ye're rather secluded at Dunrangour." Coburn shrugged and resumed his sensual onslaught on her hand and wrist. "The news didna reach ye yet. That's all."

She well understood lingering grief. Mum yet mourned Da, and often her eyes still misted with sorrow. But Da had been a wonderful, loving father and husband, while Artair Rutherford...

Blast her stays, but a slow, heady fire tunneled through Mayra's veins. Deucedly difficult to concentrate on the important subject when her very bones were in danger of melting.

She swallowed and, with some effort, she focused on the topic at hand. "Still, I would've thought Rutherford would have sent us word of somethin' of such importance. Just another instance of his flagrant disregard, I suppose."

Would Logan be less inclined to grant her request or more, now that he was Lockelieth's laird? The emotional storm raging inside her exceeded the unrelenting tempest thrashing the Highlands.

"Mayra, what makes ye think breakin' the betrothal will raise King George's ire?"

At Coburn's soft question, she veered her attention from the tumultuous outdoors.

She sighed and peaked her brows high on her forehead for a resigned instant. "The king must approve the termination. Or if he winna, then Rutherford must be the one to cry off. I canna."

"Because...?" Coburn would have the whole torrid tale, it seemed.

Mayra finally withdrew her hand when Searc began lighting additional lamps and candles about the dim room. She'd been too bold already, and to continue to permit Coburn to fondle her hand atop the table was pure foolishness, no matter how splendid it might feel.

"It's nae a pretty tale, Coburn. At least no' the portion I've been told. But I have nae cause to doubt my parents."

The gentle upward melding of his lips spread tenderness across the carved planes of his dear face. Encouragement shone in his kind gaze. He was the type of man she could love, the type who tempted her to pelt responsibility and reason to next December.

And beyond.

"Tell me, Mayra. I want to ken everythin' about ye."

After an indecisive moment, she gave a small, reluctant nod. "I dinna wish to speak ill of the dead. But Artair Rutherford was a covetous cur, as well as an intimate confident of King William."

Coburn frowned, twin lines crinkling his forehead from temple to temple and drawing his taut mouth into a stern line. "Why do ye believe that?"

"Rutherford whispered falsehoods in King William's ear about my da's loyalty to the Crown. He went so far as to produce witnesses attestin' they'd heard Da's treasonous murmurings." A thread of bitterness seeped into her words. "All fabricated, paid-for lies, of course. But Da's great uncle *had* conspired decades before, and he swung from the gallows for his treachery."

All a rouser needed to stir fear was a strand of truth, no matter how farfetched and false the nefarious accusation.

Tense lines framing his mouth, Coburn rested his forearms on the table.

Maybe she shouldn't have revealed this ugliness. Perchance it was too soon. Or, perhaps, too off-putting.

"Please, go on," he prompted, just the merest bit of something—pain or regret?—deepening his voice.

"Mum said hatred and greed motivated Artair Rutherford to falsely accuse Da. To prove his loyalty to King William, my father was forced to agree to betroth me to Logan Rutherford. If he refused, Da faced imprisonment and confiscation of Dunrangour

Tower." Ire rang in her whispered words. "That would've left Mum and me destitute."

Unnaturally still, even guarded, Coburn regarded her keenly. Not accusing, exactly, but definitely assessing. "But why go to such efforts? Only a mon with a vendetta or one unhinged takes those measures, and I dinna believe Rutherford was off his head."

Mayra smoothed an eyebrow, then touched two fingers to her chin, searching her memory for the details.

"At one time, Artair Rutherford had been betrothed to Da's sister, and the same valuable property dowered to me had also been a part of Aunt Astrid's settlement. I dinna believe it was mere chance my settlement included the same acres. Artair verra specifically demanded that provision both times."

Listening intently, Coburn's eyes narrowed until only the irises showed. "Is the property especially valuable?"

Mayra hitched one shoulder and rubbed her hands over her arms when another gust seeped through the inn's siding. "I dinna really ken. Supposedly, years ago, someone found evidence of copper and silver ore. Da always said he planned to explore the possibility of minin' the crags before he was forced to settle the land on me. He couldna touch it afterward."

"Why didna Artair and Astrid marry?" Coburn tapped his long fingers atop the table, his expression bland.

So, why did she have the impression he fumed inwardly? Mayhap she'd made a huge mistake in telling him everything.

Well, if this put him off, then he wasn't the man she'd believed. He might as well know the rest, and then she'd know if she'd misjudged him after all.

She'd hoped—*believed*—he might not care about the unsavory rumors and whispers shadowing the Findlays for generations.

Such disenchantment engulfed Mayra, she feared she might be ill, and she took a hasty gulp of tepid tea to wash the bitterness from her mouth.

"A mere month before their weddin', Astrid eloped with a gypsy traveler," Mayra said. "The notes she sent Artair and our family said she loved the traveler and carried his bairn. She died givin' birth, and the wee bairn died too."

Mayra had learned the sordid tale when Da lay dying.

He'd begged her to forgive him for promising her to Logan Rutherford.

Of course, she'd forgiven him. He'd only tried to protect her and Mum. And later, his sons.

"So ye believe revenge motivated the elder Rutherford to falsely accuse yer father and force him to agree to troth ye to Logan?" Something like pained disbelief frayed the edges of Coburn's lowered voice.

She slanted her head and shied her brows upward in affirmation.

"Aye. I do. Revenge and greed. Artair Rutherford maintained Aunt Astrid's settlement was his since their betrothal was never terminated before she died. There was nae legal basis for his claim, and accordin' to my parents, he was infuriated when denied the property."

"It seems there's a great deal about Artair Rutherford I never kent." Jaw taut, Coburn skimmed his fingers over his strong chin and veered his troubled gaze outside, now enclosed in night's garments as nature continued to wreak her havoc.

Several lengthy, silent moments passed as he remained absorbed in whatever thoughts consumed him. Mayra wrestled with her decision to share all.

Had it been a disastrous mistake?

Suppressing the despondency rising high from her belly, and emboldened by her decision to pioneer her own destiny, she cleared her throat. Her voice a mere husky shred, she murmured, "I confess, I'm grateful for yonder wicked weather if it means I might enjoy yer company longer."

Coburn's mouth swept upward, tenderness softening his handsome features.

"And I yers. Please, join me before the fire, and tell me of this plan of yers to escape Rutherford."

13

L ogan withdrew his watch and examined the face in the dancing firelight.

Nearly half-past one.

The MacPhersons and the other guests had long since retired, and even the storm waned as if spent from the hours of assaulting the earth in its furious tantrum.

Delicate moonbeams stretched outward from the crisp moon, all the more brilliant in the ebony, storm-scrubbed sky.

He yawned behind one hand, flicking the timepiece cover shut with the other.

Melancholy, blacker than the Earl of Hell's waistcoat, pulled his mouth downward. His father had been a covetous, manipulating blackguard. Honor, it seemed, was a rare commodity, and Logan's own behavior wasn't above reproach either.

As much as he wanted to believe everything Mayra had told him was a vast, fabricated lie, in his gut, in the depths of his soul, he knew she spoke the truth. It explained so much, yet he couldn't bring himself to hate or revile Da.

Logan grazed a hand across his bristly face and released a long, irregular breath.

"What am I to do about ye, Mayra Findlay?"

If only there were a way to make things right.

The how of it escaped him, nevertheless.

He couldn't see an alternative to the path he and Mayra had been set upon so many years ago.

Logan ran his thumbnail across the watch's silver case embossed with the family crest. The reverse side boasted the Rutherford motto: *Nec sorte, ne facto*—Neither by chance nor destiny.

His focus strayed to Mayra again, asleep on the other chair, her feet tucked beneath her and one slim hand cradling her cheek. Her full, creamy breasts surged upward, threatening to spill from her gown's bodice.

Neither by chance nor destiny.

Choice then?

Their betrothal at an age neither was old enough to understand or object to.

Their encounter that first day she'd tumbled from the cart.

Today's storm, forcing Mayra to stay in town.

Their obvious, immediate attraction to each other.

Far more by chance or destiny rather than a deliberate choice explained each of those circumstances.

And absolutely countered all that was rational.

Sitting there, watching the slow rise and fall of her chest, her slightly parted mouth, and the occasional flicker of her lashes fanning her cheeks, a peace unlike anything he'd experienced encompassed him.

The law proclaimed her already his and now, more than ever, he was determined she would be.

Her little cockeyed, elfin smile, the playful way she tilted her head when she listened, the way her eyes glowed with enthusiasm when she had something she wanted to say. Each characteristic delightful and endearing, and each wrapped him more snugly, more securely, and inescapably in the web he'd spun.

Her plan was simple and straightforward.

Create a scandal and force him to put her aside.

Except after spending the day with her, growing more enchanted by the moment with the beautiful, witty lass, that was the last thing he meant to do. More determined now than ever to make her Lady Rutherford, he weighed his options.

He had but one.

He must tell her the truth.

Tomorrow.

Logan stood and, after banking the fire, gathered their belongings. He secured everything within her arisaid, and tied the corners together into a makeshift pack. He'd retained a room for her when she went to use the necessary. It was across from his at the third floor passage's far end, where he could make sure she was safe.

Though few guests lodged at the inn tonight, he'd not take a chance.

After sliding the crook of his elbow into the loop

he'd created in the plaid, he scooped Mayra into his arms.

Although she opened her eyes for an instant, giving him a sleepy—*damn my eyes*—almost a seductive smile, after looping her slender arms around his neck, she shut her lids and resumed her contented slumber.

As he carried her up the flights, welcoming her weight and the chance to hold her close, every now and again she murmured in her sleep. Winded by the time he trudged up the last riser, he adjusted her and managed to push the latch to her door without dumping her onto the floor.

Though only just, as she tilted dangerously, and her head came within an inch of smacking the doorframe.

A womanizer, he was not, and neither had he experience toting lovely lasses to their bedchambers. He kicked the door closed and Mayra clung tighter, evidently believing the trek upstairs part of her dream.

"I've never been kissed," she sighed against his neck, her words sleep-thickened and garbled.

Her silky lips rasped against his flesh, and he flexed his jaw against the current of electric desire pounding along his veins.

He dropped Mayra's plaid on the chamber's single chair situated below the window, and in the moon's muddled half-light managed to bump his way to the bed. He tried to lay her down, but she clung to him, and in the throes of her dream, kissed his neck, then his jaw. And finally, her lips found his.

So incredibly sweet.

God help him, he shouldn't.

His pathetic honor, what remnant remained, screeched in offense.

Logan sank onto the bed, still snuggling her, and succumbed to temptation, feathering tiny kisses across her smooth brow, her silky lashes, the oh-so-sensitive tendon behind her ear.

"Coburn, kiss me. Really kiss me."

She moaned, that throaty, feminine, purr-like rumble which sent lust pounding to every pore.

He untwined her arms and, his chest heaving from self-restraint, Logan shook his head, though even if she'd been awake, she couldn't have seen much more than the shadowy movement.

"Lass, God kens I'm no' perfect, but I dinna ravish sleepin' maids."

"I'm no' asleep."

She giggled and turned onto her side. "I awoke when ye practically dumped me onto the floor." Slanting a glance to the window, she hid a delicate yawn behind her hand. "The storm has come to an end?"

The tempest outside.

The one raging within him showed no sign of abating. "Aye, and the moon has come out in all her glitterin' finery to celebrate."

He lit the single taper atop the humble nightstand, needing a moment to perform the mundane task to bring his stampeding ardor under control. He was aroused and ready, but there'd be no carnal satisfaction.

She'd never forgive him when she learned the truth tomorrow. He'd never forgive himself for taking advantage of her delicate state.

Reaching up, she traced a trembling finger along his jaw.

"I do want to kiss ye, Coburn. Verra much, in fact. Is that wrong? Does that make me wicked?"

She stilled her timid exploration and curled her finger into her fist before slowing withdrawing her hand and dropping her gaze to the flickering candle.

"I suppose it does, disna it? I'm promised to another."

Tell her the truth.

Logan caught her hand and brought it to his mouth. He brushed his lips across the knuckles. "Nae, it disna make ye wicked, lass. It makes ye young and healthy with a woman's desires."

Her luminous gaze gravitated to his. No guile or coyness shone in her beautiful blue eyes as she slanted her head in her quaint pixy way, her eyes probing to the depths of his soul.

"And do ye desire me, Coburn?"

Did he draw air to breathe?

Did he need food and water to live?

Did the moon, even now, light the heavens with

silvery brilliance, almost equal to Mayra's tumbled tresses, spilling over her shoulders and back, cascading down her arms?

"Aye, lass. I desire ye." And his heart? What was happening to that organ? Something he'd never anticipated. "The scorchin' blood in my veins sings with want for ye."

Even as he spoke, he stretched out beside her and gathered her in his embrace. Inhaling her intoxicating floral scent, he nuzzled her neck and brushed his hands over her curvaceous hips and gently sloping thighs.

Foolishness. Insanity.

Absolute, glorious stupidity.

Mayra cupped his face with her soft palm and touched her lips to his chin. "Is that what I feel for ye? This strange, unnamed yearnin'? Is that why, even though we scarcely ken each other, I canna rid my thoughts of ye, and why my stomach and heart flutter in the most peculiar manner when I'm with ye?"

How had she vocalized exactly what he experienced too, as inconceivable as that might be?

Some might call it lust, and surely carnal desire

bubbled within him. But he'd known physical hunger before, and this was something impossibly more.

He kissed her forehead, such tenderness throttling up his throat, he swallowed against the emotion.

"I think, perhaps, we've had somethin' rare and unexplainable occur, lass."

Tell her!

Mayra arched her neck, giving him access to the pearly column. "And what is that?"

Her question ended on a husky sigh when he glided his fingertips across her puckered nipple.

"I would make ye mine for all time, Mayra lass. I've fallen in love with ye. My verra soul craves yer presence. Ye make me feel whole."

The full brilliance of her smile blossomed across her face.

"Aye, and I ye, Coburn. I dinna understand how 'tis possible in so short a time, but I winna deny it." Her joy faded almost as quickly, and her pretty mouth turned down. "But I canna be with ye in that way. No' when I legally belong to another."

He took a steadying breath, prepared to tell all.

"Mayra—"

Her pleading look and the fingertips she touched to his lips muzzled him.

"I want to, believe me. I do with all my heart. It's just that my entire life it's been drilled into me that I'm Rutherford's, and though I owe him nothin'—loathe the man, truth to tell—I canna betray him in that way." Her husky voice caught on a dry sob and, turning her head away, she pressed the fingertips of the other hand to her lips.

Happiness, bittersweet and pungent, wrapped around him.

God, how he loved her for her faithfulness. Yet part of him wanted her to hurl common sense and restraint aside and give herself to him despite the rashness or certain repercussions.

He kissed the fingers touching his mouth before gathering her near.

"Ah, my love. My precious love. All will be well. Somehow, I vow, I shall make it so," Logan said. "Now sleep. I'll watch over ye and leave before first light so nae tongues wag."

Then for God's sake, mon, tell her the damned truth!

Logan couldn't.

Not yet.

Not now.

Mayra loathed Rutherford.

No.

She loathed *him.*

14

Twice during the night Mayra awoke, each time nestled securely in Coburn's solid, wonderfully-scented embrace, his shoulder pillowing her head. She smiled and cuddled closer, hardly daring to believe this marvelous specimen of manhood loved her.

Seems 'twas her fate to love a Highland rogue after all.

What a magnificent destiny.

Chin resting on her cupped hand, she gloried in the luxury of examining him as he slept.

Hair mussed, his dark lashes fanning his high cheeks, he appeared younger, contented. Yet, what did she know of this stranger who'd so easily captured her heart?

In all their conversations, he'd never even

revealed what brought him to Glenliesh.

Wisdom demanded she at least discover something more than he was an only child and had no kin, save a dear cousin, and that he'd traveled these three years past. But then again, wisdom, for all its benefits, didn't have a heart or soul. And therefore, wisdom couldn't possibly conceive how people knew when they'd found their mates.

The third time she wakened, the sun shone bright in the morning sky, and Coburn's side of the bed was empty.

Heavens!

She bolted upright and shook her hair off her shoulders.

What time was it?

Through the window, she studied the sun's placement and scrutinized the cloudless heavens once more.

Mayhap eight?

The hour wasn't so very advanced then, but later than her typical six o'clock rising time.

That was what came of staying up and talking

until the wee morning hours. She climbed from the bed and, stretching her arms overhead, smiled with pure joy. Her mouth remained tipped upward as she futilely attempted to smooth her wrinkled gown.

Coburn had left as promised, more concerned with her reputation than she.

If he'd been discovered in the chamber with her, surely Rutherford would've called off the wedding. Her reputation would've been shredded, of course. But what did that matter when Coburn wanted to marry her?

Except—

He hadn't actually said that he wanted to wed her. Only that he loved her and wanted to make her his.

Had she made a colossal mistake in judgement last night, sharing a bed, no matter how innocent?

What if...

She could scarcely form the thought.

What if he were married already?

God, why hadn't that occurred to her before?

Nae. Nae!

She wouldn't believe it of him.

Coburn could've taken advantage of her.

She'd wanted him to, and yet after she'd explained why she couldn't be intimate with him, he'd acted the gentleman. Well, fine, perhaps not a perfect gentleman, because he could've as easily slept outside her door, but he hadn't imposed himself on her.

More's the pity.

She chuckled and, arms extended, spun in a gleeful circle.

What a wanton she'd become.

After washing her face and rinsing her teeth, she ran her fingers through her wild tresses.

No use.

She normally plaited her hair before sleeping. The best she could hope for was to constrain the mass. As she tried to find her scattered hair pins, then bring the springy curls that called themselves her hair under control, she worried her lower lip.

What about the dowry?

Was it forfeit if she was disgraced?

Ballocks and bluebells.

Why hadn't she considered that before?

She'd never read the dafty settlement. Everything—*everything*—hinged on the dowered portions being returned to Dunrangour.

As soon as she returned home, she needed to read the contract.

Worrying her lower lip, she strolled to the window and scanned the horizon. She should be on her way soon.

Mum and Bettie, and the boys too, would've worked themselves into a proper worry by now. In fact, Mum had likely dispatched clansmen to the village already. Surprising she hadn't sent them last night, truth be told.

Except, she'd known Mayra always visited Maggi MacPherson, and sometimes, more often than she ought since Da died, Mum indulged in laudanum a bit too freely. She mightn't have realized Mayra hadn't returned home until this morning.

If only Mayra dared defy the edict and marry another like Aunt Astrid had.

By all the wriggling eels in Loch Tolhorf, that would solve the dowry problem. But then, what became of Dunrangour? Mum and the boys?

Would King George punish them and Coburn too?

From his pompous English throne, would His Majesty care in the least about two Highland clans' issues?

She heaved a frustrated sigh. The risk to them was simply too great to take.

A soft knock interrupted her unsettled musings.

"Aye? Come in."

Coburn, his hair damp and his green eyes snapping with happiness, stepped partway inside. "I have breakfast awaitin' us below. Then I'll accompany ye home. I must speak with yer mum."

"Why?" Mayra paused in collecting her arisaid hanging over the chair's back.

Coburn cocked his head boyishly, a teasing grin crimping his mouth.

"Why do I have breakfast below?"

"Nae, why do ye want to speak with my mum, ye daft *mon*?" Laughing, she threw a pillow at him, and he ducked.

"Because I intend to ask her for yer hand in marriage."

Jaw unhinged and mouth gone dry, Mayra went still as stone.

Oh, if only it could be so.

"It's no' possible without the king's consent, Coburn."

"It *is* possible. Will ye trust me, *leannan*?"

Sweetheart.

She swallowed and gave a short, uncertain nod.

As he touched her cheek and traced a path to her lips, his penetrating gaze sent a message she couldn't understand before he drew her into his arms and whispered in her unruly hair.

"Mayra, there's somethin' I should've told ye when we first met. Somethin' I've tried to tell ye many times."

She shut her eyes, swathed in contentment and savoring the precious moment until rapid hoof beats, stampeding into the village, drew her attention to the small window.

Aye, indeed. Mum was in a right royal fuss and froth.

Six Dunrangour clansmen trotted their mounts

straight to The Dozing Stag.

"My clansmen are here. I'd expected as much."

If she stayed in this chamber with Coburn, she'd have her scandal.

Indecision plucked her nerves like taut harp strings before she filled her lungs with a revitalizing breath.

Mayra whirled away from him and the window.

She couldn't so easily bring disgrace on the Findlay name and her clan after all.

So she'd give Coburn his chance with Mum and then, if that failed, only then would she resort to ruination.

Draping her arisaid about her shoulders, she hurried to the door. "Ye can call this afternoon. I'll try to prepare Mum. Though be warned, she'll no' easily be swayed. She's lived in fear for so long, I dinna think she'll be amenable."

"Mayra, wait." His face taut, Coburn held out his hand, palm upward. "There's somethin' important I really must tell ye."

The echo of booted feet hammering up the stairs

filtered into the chamber.

"Miss Mayra?" a familiar voice called.

Fergus, Dunrangour's war chief, and Da's closest friend.

She sent Coburn a panicked glance.

"It's all right." He came to her and, after clasping her hand, offered a reassuring smile. "We'll face them together."

Och, nae help for it now.

Scandal and disgrace was upon her. Chin up and shoulders squared, she'd face her ruination boldly.

Mayra backed away from the door a few paces. "I'm in here, Fergus."

Coburn squared his shoulders and notched his chin upward as well, like a general about to enter the battlefield.

Fergus and Hamish crowded into the chamber, stopping short upon spying Coburn. Fergus' wary gaze sank to Mayra's fingers entwined with Coburn's.

"By Odin's bones, ye're the verra last person I expected to see," Fergus said, his eyes wide with astonishment and disbelief.

Eyes faintly squinted, Mayra swung her gaze from man to man. "Ye ken each other?"

Not impossible. She just hadn't anticipated it. More fool she.

"Aye." Hamish tilted his head a fraction, appearing none too pleased at the admittance. "I'd have recognized ye anywhere, Rutherford. Even if it has been nigh on to three-and-a-half years since I was banished by yer sire from settin' foot on Lockelieth's land again."

Oh, for goodness' sake. They've confused Coburn for Logan.

To alleviate Fergus' and Hamish's scowls, Mayra withdrew her hand from Coburn's.

"Ye're mistaken, Hamish," Mayra said. "He's Coburn Wallace, no' Rutherford."

She finished securing the Luckenbooth brooch at her breast for the last time. After this morning, she'd never wear it again. It would be returned to Rutherford.

Fergus' grizzly eyebrows made a slow ascent up his broad forehead, and he cast Coburn an accusatory glare. "Nae, lass, he isna. He's Logan Rutherford. I'd swear my life on it. Coburn Wallace be his cousin."

15

A lethargic fog engulfed Mayra, slowing her heartbeat, muffling her hearing, distorting her vision. In trance-like disbelief, she blinked and shook her head.

Surely she'd heard wrong.

Fergus hadn't vowed Coburn was Rutherford? Had he?

As in Logan Rutherford.

Her betrothed.

Oh, God, nae. Please dinna let it be so.

She jerked her head to look at Coburn, seeing the answer in his grim countenance and speaking, entreating gaze.

He'd been impersonating his cousin.

She closed her eyes against the entreaty in his.

Charlatan! Liar!

"Please, Mayra. Let me explain."

He reached for her hand again, but she tucked her arms tight to her chest and retreated a pair of steps.

"Aye, somebody better be about explainin'," Hamish grumbled, his arms akimbo as he exchanged a severe glance with Fergus. "Yer mum's frantic, and she didna mention anythin' about yer meetin' yer betrothed in the village."

His eyes, usually a toasty brown, narrowed a wee bit, just this side of condemnation.

"That's 'cause she didna ken, did she, lass?" Fergus' gentle question hung suspended.

No, Mum didn't know. But neither had Mayra.

Nonetheless, she realized how guilty she and Co— Logan appeared. If she'd been able to draw a decent breath, she'd have laughed at the irony.

Clandestine meetings with her affianced.

The stuff of sordid tales.

And what's more, she'd stupidly, *stupidly* fallen in love with him. A man she'd convinced herself was a worthless sot.

He's nae a worthless sot.

He's a lyin' scunner.

Deceiver. Cawker. Scoundrel. Rogue.

And, to her absolute consternation, even amidst his gut-wrenching treachery, he was still the man she loved with every excruciating breath she drew. One's heart didn't stop loving someone simply because their name changed.

However, it could, in the span of a heartbeat, stop trusting and believing.

After commanding her thoughts and stomach to cease their pitching, she inhaled a great gulp of fortifying air. Gradually releasing it, she angled her head.

"Hamish, Fergus, would ye please give me a moment alone with..."

Mayra couldn't call him Logan.

In her mind, he was still Coburn.

From the corner of her eye, she saw the frown framing his firm mouth and the lines creasing his forehead over the slightly hooded gaze regarding her.

"Please give us a moment alone," she managed,

righteous anger giving her strength.

Flinty faces unyielding, neither of her clansmen seemed inclined to move a muscle of their hulking, imposing forms.

Another time, she might have appreciated their protectiveness. But not when the tight rein she held on her composure threatened to plummet over the humiliating precipice of hysterics.

"Ye may wait in the passageway outside the door. I'll only be a few moments."

Mayra would have her say with...Logan.

How could she ever become accustomed to that name for him?

She'd harbored resentment for so long, and it had colored Logan Rutherford as a heartless, selfish knave. Her mind couldn't reconcile that personality with the marvelous man before her that she'd come to know and love.

"I give my word as a Scot, she has nothin' to fear from me." Logan unflinchingly met her champions' stony gazes.

Nothing in their steely countenances yielded a jot.

"Five minutes is all I require," he said, his expression every bit as unyielding.

To do what?

"I am still her betrothed," Logan reminded them, a trifle more force behind his words. "It is my legal right."

God rot his handsome face, he was.

Their reluctance as obvious as their disapproval, Fergus and Hamish shuffled from the room, then shut the door behind their broad backs.

Mayra hadn't a doubt they stood directly outside the door. They probably had their ears pressed to the coarse slats, truth be told.

Both had looked ready to pound Rutherford to next March. She'd like to clout him in his aristocratic nose too.

Pain radiating from her core in undulating waves, Mayra wandered to the window and, after presenting her stiff back, pressed her fingers between her eyes for a moment.

She wouldn't cry.

Nonetheless, such agony burgeoned from her

belly, traveling up her constricted chest and tight throat, she could hardly summon one anguished, whispered word.

"Why?"

"Mayra, my precious bonnie lass." Emotion deepened the timbre of Logan's voice.

He crossed to stand behind her, a tempting wall of virile masculinity. The heat of his body enshrouded her as did his scent.

Then he settled his big, yet wonderfully gentle hands on her shoulders. Rather than railing her indignation, she yearned to turn into his embrace and weep like a bairn.

Instead, she stiffened her spine and shoulders and shrugged off his hands. Out of self-preservation, she kept her back to him. For if she looked into his eyes, those mesmerizing hazel pools, she feared she'd weaken and succumb to her feckless heart.

And right now, this instant, her mind and her indignation insisted on answers.

"Why?"

She sent the briefest of glances over her shoulder

before gripping the windowsill, her knuckles white from the pressure.

"I need to understand why ye deceived me, Logan, when the truth would've served us both so much better."

"Because I'm an idiot. I kent ye desperately wanted out of the betrothal, and I couldna honor yer request." Logan's long sigh warmed her nape, he stood so close.

Couldn't or wouldn't?

A vast difference between the two. "Why no'?"

"My da spent the dowry entrusted to his care. I dinna have the monies to replace it. In fact, Lockelieth totters on financial ruin. To save her, we must wed verra soon, so I can claim the rest of the dowry."

Nae.

Mouth parted in shock and dismay, Mayra whipped around.

"He spent it? *All* of it?" she whispered through the tightness choking her throat. "And Lockelieth still faces ruin. How can that be?"

Scorching, stubborn tears welled, but just as

obstinately, she blinked them away.

She understood full well what this meant. Damn Artair Rutherford's corrupt soul. May he burn in hell for all time.

Outraged fury wrestled with reason until common sense, heavily tinged with bitterness, prevailed.

"Ye could've simply told me as much, Logan. Been honest with me. At least after the first time we met. But to carry on the charade..."

Mayra shook her head and several curls toppled loose.

Stupid, diddy hair. She'd cut it off above her ears!

He caught one tendril between his fingers and tugging it ever so gently, pulled her into his arms.

Outside the door, the floorboards squeaked, and a wry smile quirked one side of her mouth.

Fergus and Hamish were certainly experiencing an earful.

"Ye're right. And in hindsight, my excuse seems feeble. Even to me. I ken that now. I meant to tell ye. I was stupid and weak and a fool." His nostrils flared before he pressed a tender kiss to her forehead. "But...I was afraid."

Her brawny, powerful Highland rogue afraid?

"Of what? That I couldna love the real ye? Ye never gave me a chance to do so. What we have"—Mayra waffled her hand between them—"has been built on a lie. I dinna ken what's real anymore."

She felt violated and exposed. But worst of all, she'd been made to admit to herself that she couldn't trust her instincts.

What was she to do now?

Her greatest hope of returning Dunrangour to prosperity had been blasted to smithereens, as had any hope of nullifying their betrothal.

And even that notion had her thoughts tumbling about in confusion.

Vulnerability she'd never seen before shadowed Logan's face. He shifted his attention over her head to gaze outside, and his throat worked for a moment before he spoke again.

"Aye, I dreaded ye'd loathe me, Mayra. But more than that, I feared yer loyalty, feared to trust ye. Then I fell in love with ye, and above all else, that terrified me to my marrow. Love bewitches and befuddles, makes even the most decent, logical of men do stupid, rash, asinine things."

Two heavy raps rattled the door, demanding her attention, and she tossed a frustrated glance over shoulder.

"It's been more than five minutes," Fergus said, his tone just short of a growl.

"Just a few more moments." She cocked her head at Logan's cynicism. "Ye make love sound like a putrid disease to be avoided."

Logan veered her a swift, sidelong glance before returning his perusal to the street filling with villagers going about their daily routines.

"My father's wife betrayed him with countless men. Rodena bore a wee lass, Isla, that wasna a product of my father's loins. I was determined no' to allow my emotions to rule my head and turn me into a lovesick dobber as he had. He lost sight of all that he valued. His integrity, his honor, his self-respect. She destroyed him. It was Rodena who convinced Da to squander yer dowry."

Even with her heart fragmented, her soul battered

from his duplicity, Mayra understood Logan's reluctance, although she couldn't agree with his reasoning.

"I dinna believe love does that to everyone. Perhaps those with weak, spineless characters." Which Artair Rutherford had proven he possessed. "But love also has the ability to strengthen. To fortify. To encourage greatness. My parents' marriage was a perfect example of that."

"Aye. Ye're right. It's difficult and painful to admit my father wasna the mon I thought he was." He met her gaze and his was resolute. "But I vow to ye, I am no' him."

"And I'm no' yer stepmum." Hadn't she demonstrated her virtuousness already?

A wry half-smile quirked Logan's mouth upward on one side. "Can I ask why ye've been so determined to end our betrothal? Is it because ye didna want to marry a stranger, or is there somethin' more?"

Mayra hunched a shoulder an inch, sadness and marrow-deep disappointment a heavy mantle upon her.

"It was partially because I didna want to marry a

mon I didna ken. One I mistakenly believed a callous churl." She cut him a contrite glance.

"Mayra—"

She raised her palm to him. "Please. Let me finish."

"Aye. Go on then," Logan said.

"I've never been a silly female who dreamed of a knight or a prince carryin' her off on a white horse to live blissfully ever after." She tucked a curl behind her ear, her attention beyond the window. "But since Da died, it's been because I couldna fathom another way to save Dunrangour except to use the dowry. However, unlike the portion trusted to yer father's care, the other half has remained intact. We never spent a single coin."

Logan touched her shoulder for a brief moment. "I believe I have a solution for that, which would also help the villagers and restore Lockelieth. I want to start a minin' venture on the land that's part of yer settlement."

"That's a lofty goal." And though noble, it did little to appease her profound disenchantment.

Excitement lit his countenance and eagerness inflected his voice. "I believe the adjacent acres are also silver and copper-rich. I've had a letter from my cousin who says there are also tin and coal deposits in the region. We'd need the rest of yer dowry to start the undertakin', but I've also several investments that I hope will begin producin' a solid income within a year."

"Ye've thought this out, it seems."

If what Logan said were true, then at least she didn't have to fear for Dunrangour's or her family's futures.

Just her own, which looked precarious at best.

Logan brought her hands to his mouth and pressed his lips for a long moment to first the knuckles of one hand, then the other.

"Can ye forgive me, Mayra? Give our love a chance? Let me make amends? Prove that ye can trust me?"

"Forgive ye? Aye. In time, I have nae doubt I can. I dinna hold grudges. However, trust ye? Nae. That I canna vow. Trust canna be rekindled as simply as puttin' a spark to tinder." She snapped her fingers before his face, permitting her hurt to speak.

He bowed his neck. "Ye're right, of course."

"And I believe a marriage without trust, even an arranged one, is worse than a union without love. I've been forthright with ye from the verra beginnin', Logan. I told ye I was betrothed. I told ye I'd considered creatin' a scandal." She lowered her voice so Fergus and Hamish couldn't hear her confession. "I didna give myself to ye because my honor wouldna permit it."

"And I love ye all the more for each of those. I ken I dinna deserve ye. Nevertheless, please, believe me when I say that above all else, I would make ye my wife. No' because a paper says we must, but because I canna imagine my life without ye now."

Entreaty and sincerity sharpened the contours of Logan's dear face, but the moisture filling the corners of his eyes nearly undid Mayra.

Yet, for weeks he'd lied, and that she couldn't easily forget or put aside. She respected herself too much.

Righteous anger prompted her words, even as the door shuddered when either Hamish or Fergus bumped it.

"For all of yer pretty professions, unless His Majesty releases us, ye ken as well as I that I've nae choice but to wed ye." Mayra was right back where she started mere weeks ago, only now her heart was no longer her own.

An auburn-haired rogue, whether he deserved it or not, had laid claim to the bruised organ.

One hand on his nape, Logan tucked his head to his chest, remaining silent for a long moment before raising his gaze to snare hers. "Aye, what ye say is true. Tell me what ye would have me do then, sweet lass? Naught but yer happiness matters to me. I shall write King George too, if that is what ye wish, though we both ken he mightna even respond."

The door trembled again.

For certain, the great gollumpuses waiting in the corridor could use a dose of patience.

Mayra stepped away from Logan and, after gathering her gloves and hat, faced him.

"My emotions are flyin' too high at present to make a rational decision. I need time to think, to contemplate the best course."

To determine if I dare trust ye ever again.

"I shall give ye my answer when I return from Edinburgh."

16

Edinburgh
April 1720

Sitting at her dressing table, Mayra cracked the green wax seal. She managed to wait until she was alone in her chamber to read Logan's most recent letter.

If only he'd made this much effort to write to her before. To woo her. To create something between them.

Breathing out a long sigh, she blinked tears from her eyes that thinking of him always caused.

The weeks apart hadn't lessened her love for the rogue, more fool she.

The foolscap crackled softly as she unfolded the paper, then ran her fingertips over the crisp page. He'd touched this same surface with his strong, callused hands.

If she closed her eyes, she could still feel his fingers trailing across her cheek. She touched her mouth. And still feel his firm, warm, wonderful lips upon hers.

Her eyes misted, and she released another ragged sigh as she slowly opened them.

My Dearest Mayra,

I pray this letter finds ye well, at least in form, if no' spirit. I'm no' surprised ye havena responded to my previous missives, but I shallna give up so easily. I believe with all my heart we are meant to be together. Please allow me to prove myself to ye.

I wrote ye a poem. I ken women like such things.

My Love
Eyes the color of the summer sky
Fair skin smooth and pearly white
Bowed lips, plump and strawberry red
Hair shimmerin' moonbeam bright

Yer faithful, lovin', humble servant,
L

A smile twitching the corners of her mouth, Mayra

slowly refolded the letter before adding it to the growing stack in her dressing table's drawer.

Poetry wasn't Logan's forte, but she adored him for the effort.

Skin pearly white, indeed.

Maybe...

Maybe he deserved a second chance.

~*~

A glass of sparkling wine in hand and one chain mail-covered shoulder propped against a marble column, Logan adjusted his itchy black mask for the umpteenth time as he scrutinized the ballroom, paralleled on two sides by gilded mirrors.

Seeking Mayra, he gulped down the tepid wine and swung his gaze toward the doors leading to the garden.

Too cold to venture out there tonight, even if a smattering of spring color dotted the well-ordered beds.

Still, he had a groom with a white horse waiting before the mansion.

Just in case...

His gaze roved the crowd once more. For the

tenth? Twentieth time?

Where was she? Coburn said Mayra wore a medieval maiden's gown of the palest blue adorned with silver netting.

Over four weeks had passed since she'd left Logan standing in The Dozing Stag, wondering if he'd truly destroyed his only chance at love and happiness. He'd spent more than thirty sleep-deprived nights, flopping about his lonely bed, pummeling himself with recriminations.

He'd written her twice weekly, something he should've done long before.

In those missives, he'd apologized over and over, told her of his love, his plans for their future, and he begged her to give them a chance, to forgive him. He'd even written a sorry excuse for a poem.

She hadn't responded.

Not to a single correspondence.

Had she even received the missives?

He'd rather believe she hadn't than that she'd ignored his letters.

As hers had been unheeded for months—no years.

Finally, unable to lounge about Lockelieth any longer without going *off his head* from frustration, his mind constantly straying to Mayra, Logan decided on a new course.

One that might fail, but which wouldn't have him twiddling his thumbs and moping about the keep. He must prove himself to her. Somehow convince her he'd never be so bloody stupid or deceitful again.

He searched the crowded room for the umpteenth time.

Guests in an enormous variety of costumes from creative to ridiculous—was Lord Fowler supposed to be a chicken or a turkey?—stepped in time to a Scottish reel or gossiped in small clusters, wine or punch glasses clasped in their gloved hands.

Others—mostly shy wallflowers and drowsy elderly dames—perched in the chairs lining the room's one end. And still more revelers wandered the perimeter, their countenances intense and searching.

Is that how he looked?

Almost desperate and yet hopeful too?

Did they, too, seek a beloved?

Or perhaps, their love unrequited, they merely sought a glimpse of the object of their affections?

Coburn swore he'd observed Mayra dancing a strathspey earlier, but although Logan had kept a hawk's eye on the milling throng, he'd seen nary a glimpse of a female with moonlight threaded through her locks, an enchanting pixyish smile on her rosy mouth, and the sky dancing in her merry blue eyes.

"Ye're moonin', Cousin. I should dub ye Sir Dour, Knight of the Gloomy Realm." Coburn chuckled as he once again eyed Logan's costume up and down.

A bland look was Logan's only response to his cousin's needling.

"I still canna fathom why ye're dressed as a knight. Every time ye move, ye clink and clank worse than a black tinker's wagon. How do ye propose to dance, or piss for that matter, in that contraption?" He flicked a long finger at Logan's armor, mirth cavorting in his merry gaze, visible through his mask's eye slits.

A skeptical brow elevated, Logan eyed his cousin's swashbuckler's attire, his dark red hair held in place by a dashing blue scarf.

"At least I chose a respectable profession."

"Och, trust me, Cousin, the lasses dinna always want a respectable chap. Sometimes they want a *mon* to scoop them into their arms, whisk them away, and steal a kiss." Smirking, he gave a wicked wink. "And sometimes sample a wee bit more of their bountiful charms too."

"Ever the romantic. Some women do like bein' treated with respect and reverence, ye ken." Logan's droll response earned him a whoop of laughter.

"Dear cousin, ye are completely, absolutely besotted." Coburn's grin couldn't be described as anything other than gloating.

"Just ye wait, Coburn. Yer day may come yet," Logan said. "And if it does, I'll be right there mockin' ye, rubbin' yer nose in yer warmer affections."

Coburn threw his hands across his chest in theatric horror. "Bite yer tongue. My day will never come. Unlike ye, I'm no' obligated to produce an heir."

"I assure ye, my determination to win Mayra, despite my earlier stupidity, has nothin' whatsoever to do with obligation." Casting his cousin a look just this side of exasperated, Logan stretched his neck and scoured the crowd.

Probably look like a damned crane.

A burgundy-and-gold liveried servant passed by, and Coburn snatched two more glasses of wine. After passing one to Logan, he took a deep swallow, then made a face. "Weak as milk. I ken for a fact, McCullough has a stash of whisky and French brandy in his study. What say we help ourselves to a tot or two?"

Logan surveyed the ballroom once more.

No Mayra.

Mayhap she'd heard he was here and had fled?

Logan's stomach and heart dove to his booted feet, heavier and swifter than an anchor chucked over a schooner's side met the river's bottom.

Still, he wasn't ready to quit the field just yet.

"Ye go on ahead, Coburn. I'm goin' to wander around and try to find my betrothed."

How he adored saying that, declaring she was his. Even if it were only true for a short while longer.

Tonight, he'd know her preference, one way or the other.

Unless Mayra had truly left already.

Odin's toenails.

He should've considered the possibility. However, if she had indeed departed, he had his answer. Just not the one he'd wanted.

"Never thought the day would come that ye'd be ballocks over chin in love. And honestly, I'm utterly terrified that I, too, may someday become so ensnared." Coburn gave a much-exaggerated shudder. "Aye, a stiff quaff is most definitely in order. Mayhap more than one."

With a jaunty wave, he headed toward one of the entrances, but halfway to his destination, he veered toward a stunning raven-haired female pirate.

Lips twitching, Logan pointed his gaze ceilingward and shook his head.

Mayhap sooner than ye think, Cousin.

Methodically strolling the ballroom's border, he kept watching for a vision in blue and silver. Asking acquaintances if they'd seen her would only raise questions and possibly make things more awkward for Mayra, so he elected to keep his own counsel.

Nonetheless, he'd been here a full thirty minutes without a single glimpse of her, and that didn't bode well.

He passed the terrace windows reflecting the glow of hundreds of candles and, after glancing through the panes and assuring himself no one loitered outside, except for the willing groom paid very well to stand with Logan's noble steed, he continued on to the card room.

He swiftly perused the occupants.

Not there either.

Hands on his hips, he blew out a frustrated breath.

Devil it.

Where *was* his love?

In a carriage trundling to the Windlespoons' manor?

Was he truly too late?

The fine hairs on his nape stood up as if electrified, and he slowly turned around.

There Mayra stood, slightly uncertain, but beyond exquisite at the top of the fan-shaped stairway. Someone had tamed her wild mane, and it hung to her waist in silky waves. A circlet of diamonds graced her forehead and the choker at her neck.

A dozen swains rushed to the bottom riser, all jabbering and posturing for her attention.

Jealousy, scorching and swift, heated his blood.

A fleeting smile touched her mouth, but Logan didn't miss the discomfiture in her eyes.

She was wholly out of her element.

Striding across the marbled floor, his boots clacking and his armor jangling, he never took his attention from her.

Upon hearing his rackety approach, she turned her head, and a radiant smile of relief blossomed across her face.

She'd recognized him. Surely that meant something.

The bucks vying for her attention noticed her focus and turned disgruntled expressions his way.

One chap, dressed as a jester, nudged another attired in...

A frog costume?

They both turned bland stares on Logan, smirking at his ill-fitting armor.

He pushed his way through her admirers, perhaps using his elbows a trifle more exuberantly than necessary.

A tall, striking Roman centurion sporting a beaklike nose and haughty countenance blocked the stairs. Surveying Logan's over-sized breastplate, he sneered.

"It appears you had difficulty finding a costume that fit," he said, his clipped British accent almost as austere as the brows rising impossibly higher on his forehead. "Last minute decision to attend?"

"Ye might say that." Logan shrugged, his full attention focused on the vision floating down the stairs, her gaze locked with his.

Beak-nosed man noticed and tried to step in front of him. "Who are you, sir, that you so brazenly stare at our fair Miss Findlay?"

"I can answer that, Lord Strudwick." Mayra's musical, husky voice drew the men's attention. "He is Logan Rutherford, Laird of Lockelieth Keep. And he is my betrothed."

Hope sprang anew in Logan's chest.

Did she mean it?

He stepped forward and offered her his arm.

Resting her fingertips upon his forearm, Mayra swept the peeved men a winsome smile.

"If ye'll excuse us?" She bent her head at a

conspiratorial angle. "We've weddin' details to discuss."

Grumbling their disappointment, the men wandered away.

Logan raised her hand and, searching her eyes, kissed her fingertips. "Never have I beheld such magnificence. I wanted to punch them all for darin' to look upon yer loveliness."

Head tipped, she searched his face. "I'm surprised to see ye, Logan. Ye didna mention comin' to Edinburgh in yer letters."

Och, so she had received them. "I couldna stay away. I had to see ye, Mayra, to beg ye again to forgive me."

"We're garnerin' attention." Her bright gaze strayed beyond him.

He cast a quick glance over his shoulder. "I dinna care. Did ye mean what ye said? That we have a weddin' to plan?"

His heart stuttered in anticipation of her answer.

"Aye." She blushed, pink tinting her porcelain cheeks. "Dinna mistake me. I'm still thoroughly miffed at ye, but I love ye. And given a choice of life with ye and without, I choose ye. I would like to start over and begin our relationship anew, with both of us committed to bein' totally honest with each other."

Logan's grin would've lit the heavens; he was positive.

He didn't deserve her mercy or forgiveness, but he'd accept them with the gratefulness of a dying man given another chance at life.

"Well, then my beloved Scots lass, I've never had the opportunity to propose to ye."

He sank onto one knee, his armor clinking and clanking, then took one of her hands in his.

Her eyes rounded, and a tremulous smile framed her mouth when she caught on to what he was about.

God help him to regain his feet with a measure of decorum.

The grand entrance and the ballroom doorways filled with gaping onlookers, but Logan paid them little mind. A gradual hush spiraled outward from where he knelt, and Mayra smiled down at him, love shining in her slightly misty eyes.

"Mayra Effie Lilias Findlay, will ye take this flawed, unworthy Highlander who adores ye and give him another chance to prove to ye how utterly remarkable, delightful, and exceptional ye are?"

Her smile softened even more. "Oh, aye. I shall. I shall."

She nodded, her hair swirling about her shoulders and her smile lighting her entire countenance as he managed to stand with her assistance.

How in Hades did men fight battles wearing this device?

"I'm so happy," Mayra said. "If there werena so many people watchin' us, Logan, I'd kiss ye."

"I've nae such compunction." He swept her into his arms and, kissing her full on the mouth, trooped to the manor's exit.

A startled butler yanked the door open.

The clattering of guests' shoes, the swishing of their clothing, and the soft buzz of frenetic whispering echoed behind Logan as he continued marching down the stairs.

"I'll be jiggered!" Coburn said, clapping in

approval. "Well done ye, Cousin."

Logan sent him a smug grin.

Mayra giggled when she saw the horse. "Sir Knight, do ye mean to whisk me away on yonder steed?"

Logan set her down, just long enough to vault into the saddle.

Actually, given the unaccustomed armor encasing him, it was more of a noisy, awkward, wholly undignified arse in the air clamor, assisted by the widely grinning groom.

Logan tossed the amused chap a coin, which he promptly pocketed before cupping his hands for Mayra to step into. "M'lady?"

Light as a nymph, she deftly positioned herself sideways before Logan on the saddle. Wrapping her arms about his waist, she laid her head against his chest. "I believe we've caused a scandal."

He lowered his lips to hers once more, savoring the sweetness of her mouth she readily opened to him.

"I hope so, my love. I do hope so."

Epilogue

Lockelieth Keep
October 1720

Mayra balanced her chin on her cupped hands, watching Logan as he slept beside her. At times like this, when his masculine beauty was on full display, her heart could scarcely stand it, so full of love was she.

Oh, how she'd fought marrying him. Such bliss and joy she'd have forsaken had she succeeded in her misguided mission.

The fire she'd stoked after checking on Isla cast long, frolicking shadows across him, their bed, and onto the walls behind it.

The wee lass had come to live with her and Logan

a month ago. Isla's selfish mum remarried and couldn't be bothered with her daughter any longer. Sometimes the poor waif cried out in her sleep for her mother, as she had tonight, and Mayra comforted her until slumber claimed the sad child once more.

Mum, Bettie, and Mayra's brothers had departed for home two days ago after a lovely two-week visit. Dunrangour and Lockelieth Keeps, their people, and their lands were well taken care of now. Or at least they were well on their way to contentment.

Logan's bare, muscled chest, sprinkled with deep russet hair, tempted too much, and Mayra played her fingertips through the crispy curls. She adored running her hands over his sculpted form. Would she wake him if she kissed the tempting flesh?

He cracked an eye open, a smoldering, sleepy grin curling his mouth.

"My lady wife, are ye starin' at me again while I slumber?"

She did so often, and it had become a jest between them. "Aye. I am, my love. 'Tis yer fault for possessin' such a manly form nae woman can resist."

"Manly, eh?" His cocky smile suggested she'd awakened something else.

"Oh, aye." Mayra grinned and gave in to the impulse to kiss his chest.

She'd never tire of touching him. Of kissing him. Of loving him.

"I warned ye last time. Lasses who wake their weary husbands from a sound sleep must pay a fine. A steep fine." Logan gave a low growl and, in one deft movement, he pulled her atop his firm, molded body, then cupped her bottom in his big hands as he nibbled the sensitive arc where her shoulder met her neck.

"No' so bad a price to pay," she managed to say, passion already thrumming through her veins and turning her mind to mince.

She angled her head to give him better access, her hair forming a curtain about their heads and shoulders.

He grabbed a handful of hair and gave it a gentle tug, pulling her closer yet.

His manhood stirred beneath her belly, and she nipped his collarbone in anticipation of their joining. He groaned and lifted his pelvis, his desire thick and hot beneath her, but she wasn't ready to end their foreplay just yet.

She grasped his length, relishing his gravelly moan.

"Lass, careful, or ye'll end our sport before we've begun."

"Did I tell ye I finally received a response to my petition from King George?" She gasped when Logan brushed his palm across her breasts, lingering for a moment on each nipple.

"Did ye, now?"

He didn't seem the least interested, apparently finding her breasts more fascinating than news from their monarch.

"Aye," she managed on a breathless gasp as he plundered new sensitive territory. "Only…this…afternoon."

Yesterday, actually. The clock had chimed three a bit ago.

Logan stroked the length of her spine, his rough fingertips brushing across her bottom and upper thighs before making the reverse trek.

"And what did our illustrious Majesty say after all these months? That ye dinna have to wed me after all, lass?"

The heavy bedcovers rustled as he thrust his hips against her mons again, and she swallowed a moan of longing, then giggled when he flipped her onto her back.

"Actually, he said ye did have to honor the contract, else ye'd have to forfeit my dowry. To him."

"He didna." Eyes half-closed, Logan stopped his sensual onslaught and gave one short shake of his head. "The greedy sot."

"My thoughts as well. He'd have apoplexy if he kent we've already found copper in the mine." She nuzzled his hairy chest, drawing in a deep breath, savoring his masculine scent.

Logan waggled his eyebrows, a confident grin tilting his mouth. "Do ye suppose he'll be peeved that the deed is done and that ye're increasin' already?"

"Och, serves the pompous prig right," she said, rubbing her calf against his hairy leg. She adored the differences in their bodies. "The information Coburn found out about the minin' was invaluable to our success, wasna it?"

Every bit as charming as Logan, Coburn and his bride, Arieen, resided in the keep as well. In a very short time, she'd become the sister Mayra had never had.

"Aye. But I dinna want to discuss my cousin just now." Logan raised himself up onto his elbows and rained gentle kisses across her forehead, nose, cheeks, and, finally, a tender kiss upon her waiting mouth. "Ye ken, I'd willingly forfeit it all—Lockelieth, the mines, everythin'—if that were the cost the king demanded to keep ye at my side."

"I ken." Mayra entwined her arms about his neck and opened her legs to the gentle, insistent nudge of his knee between her thighs.

"I'd do the same for ye, without a second thought or a speck of remorse, because I love ye above all else."

"And I love ye, Mayra." As Logan slid his length home, he lowered his mouth to an inch above hers.

"Let me show ye how verra much for the rest of our lives."

About the Author

USA Today Bestselling, award-winning author COLLETTE CAMERON® scribbles Scottish and Regency historicals featuring dashing rogues and scoundrels and the intrepid damsels who reform them.Blessed with an overactive and witty muse that won't stop whispering new romantic romps in her ear, she's lived in Oregon her entire life, though she dreams of living in Scotland part-time. A self-confessed Cadbury chocoholic, you'll always find a dash of inspiration and a pinch of humor in her sweet-to-spicy timeless romances®.

Explore **Collette's worlds** at
www.collettecameron.com!

Join her **VIP Reader Club** and **FREE newsletter**.
Giggles guaranteed!

FREE BOOK: Join Collette's The Regency Rose®
VIP Reader Club to get updates on book releases,
cover reveals, contests, and giveaways she reserves
exclusively for email and newsletter followers. Also,
any deals, sales, or special promotions are offered to
club members first. She will not share your name or
email, nor will she spam you.

http://bit.ly/TheRegencyRoseGift

Follow Collette on BookBub
https://www.bookbub.com/authors/collette-cameron

From the Desk of Collette Cameron

Thank you for reading TO LOVE A HIGHLAND LAIRD. Mayra and Logan were born in a time period where arranged marriages were commonplace, as were unions dictated by the ruling monarch. To defy such an order meant death. After all, marriage was viewed as a means to gain power and position.

A contract in which children are betrothed is called a forced marriage. Unfortunately, those matches were also popular, but as you can imagine, they rarely ended happily for either party.

The marriage settlement or dowry was often used to entice a less than eager groom. A woman's worth was based on what she could bring to the marriage. She was her husband's property and was little better than a chattel.

It's no wonder Mayra was determined to end her betrothal. In a fictional novel such as TO LOVE A HIGHLAND LAIRD, norms, traditions, and customs can be modified to ensure a happy ever after. Those deviations might not be entirely historically accurate, but they make for a much more romantic read.

I hope you enjoyed Mayra and Logan's romantic adventure and that you'll read the other eight books in the Heart of a Scot series. Coburn Wallace's story is TO REDEEM A HIGHLAND ROGUE, and it is next in the series.

To stay abreast of the releases of my books and other news, you can subscribe to my newsletter (the link is below) or visit my author world at collettecameron.com.

Hugs,

Collette

Connect with Collette!

Check out her author world:

collettecameron.com

Join her Reader Group:

www.facebook.com/groups/CollettesCheris

Subscribe to her newsletter, receive a FREE Book:

www.signup.collettecameron.com/TheRegencyRoseGift

To Redeem a Highland Rogue

Heart of a Scot, Book Two

Sometimes, a kiss is only a kiss.
Meaningless. Their kiss was not that kind…

Arieen Fleming is desperate. She'll do *anything* to force her betrothed into calling off their arranged marriage—even create a public scandal that could leave her disowned, destitute, and untouchable. The charming Highlander at the masked ball is *perfect* for what she has in mind. She just had no idea how much the man—and his kiss—would change *everything* for her…

Very little is required of Coburn Wallace. As cousin and second-in-command to a laird, he doesn't need to marry or produce an heir. So when a beautiful lass dressed as a pirate demands a kiss, who is he to refuse? He never thought the impulsive act would ruin her. And he *certainly* never thought he'd eagerly step up to protect her honor with an offer of marriage. But…he did…

It was only supposed to be one kiss. Now they're bound together in a way neither intended. When all is said and done, can Arieen and Coburn find a way to turn their mutual attraction into true love? Or will their happily ever after elude them forever?

Made in the USA
Middletown, DE
05 March 2022

62145589R10121